... and artifice, the ...uisine up against the raw ...d . . . The short story is an intimate, ...: Michèle Roberts reminds us in this ...at she is one of our foremost practitioners of the ar... ...es, *Guardian*

'We are engulfed by these stories and in them, we remember our own lives' Elaine Feinstein, *Independent*

'In Michele Roberts's new collection, which contains more powerful, uncompromising writing than you will find in most novels, women's sexual consciousness and a radical perception of sexual difference hold centre stage . . . The short story is all about the ending, the point towards which the reader and the writer hurtle together. Roberts delivers her often unexpected, startling resolutions with wit and style . . . Her prose is sharp as a whip and as unforgettable as a lover's tenderness' Patricia Duncker, *Literary Review*

'Michèle Roberts draws emotional pain with precision, describing confusion with a limpid finesse' Chloe Campbell, *TLS*

'It is in the inventiveness of form and the angle at which her words are cut that Roberts still manages to dazzle . . . She takes pleasure in unpicking the fabric of fiction . . . Roberts's greatest skill is the insight with which she writes about women caught up in heightened states of awareness' Megan Walsh, *The Times*

'Entertaining, elegant, bite-sized gulps of fiction, full of lust for life' *Red*

Also by Michèle Roberts

Fiction

A Piece of the Night
The Visitation
The Wild Girl
The Book of Mrs Noah
In the Red Kitchen
Daughters of the House
During Mother's Absence
Flesh and Blood
Impossible Saints
Fair Exchange
The Looking Glass
Playing Sardines
The Mistressclass
Reader, I married him

Non-Fiction

Food, Sex & God
Paper Houses

Poetry

The Mirror of the Mother
Psyche and the Hurricane
All the Selves I Was

Artist's Books

Poems (with Caroline Isgar)
Fifteen Beads (with Caroline Isgar)
Dark City Light City (with Carol Robertson)
The Secret Staircase (with Caroline Isgar)

Michèle Roberts

mud

stories of sex and love

virago

VIRAGO

First published in Great Britain in 2010 by Virago Press
This paperback edition published in 2011 by Virago Press

A CIP catalogue record for this book
is available from the British Library.

ISBN 978-1-84408-389-3

Typeset in Garamond by M Rules
Printed and bound in Great Britain by
Clays Ltd, St Ives plc

Papers used by Virago are from well-managed forests
and other responsible sources.

MIX
Paper from
responsible sources
FSC® C104740

Virago Press
An imprint of
Little, Brown Book Group
100 Victoria Embankment
London EC4Y 0DY

An Hachette UK Company
www.hachette.co.uk

www.virago.co.uk

in memory of Monique Caulle Roberts

CONTENTS

Acknowledgments

Thanks to Ayesha Karim, Clare Alexander and everyone at Aitken Alexander Associates. Thanks to Lennie Goodings, Victoria Pepe, Sophie McIvor and everyone at Little, Brown and Virago. Thanks to Patricia Duncker, Sarah LeFanu and Jenny Newman for helpful ongoing critical feedback and discussions and for generous writerly support. Thanks to Jenny Fry, Christie Hickman, Hermione Lee and Richard Wainwright for helpful critical feedback on an earlier draft of part of this book. Thanks to all my friends and to my sister Margi Defriez and all my family.

NOTE

Earlier versions of three of these stories have been previously published and earlier versions of four have been broadcast on radio. I am grateful to the editors concerned for permission to republish these stories, which have been re-written for publication here.

Mud

Every morning I walked in to work at the university from a nearby village where I rented a room from a sad widow. I was a widow myself, in a manner of speaking (I'd run off and left my husband), but you wouldn't have known it to look at me unless you thought all women of thirty-five were in mourning. Black clothes were fashionable at that time: we all wore them. I strode in my long black mackintosh along the muddy roads edged by fields, into the great park, and thence, following a footpath, to my place of work.

Every morning I laced up my shoes; flat black suede brogues, with a thick dimpled rubber sole, a pointed triangular toe, just two eyelets, and a black lace thin as a string of liquorice that I tied into a sharp bow.

My mother frequently scolded me for my childishness: you see everything in terms of food and eating. Those black suede shoes, when I'd spotted them, furry and glistening in the shop, had indeed seemed good enough to eat. At night, when I walked back to my lodgings, to my small front bedroom in my landlady's cramped modern house, my shoes sat by the side of my single bed while I ate my bowl of spaghetti and drank my wine, and then I'd lift the shoes up, one after the other, wipe and brush them tenderly, scrape and fiddle off, with the tip of a knife, the caked mud that clotted them. Crusts clunked down, pale and dried. I liked knowing that earlier I'd left my traces along the road, that my footsteps had imprinted the scars of water-glinting gravel, the muddy ruts. In these depressions I could have cast reliefs of rubber, of plaster, of wax. I always liked seeing others' footprints, the tracks of their journeys. I liked taking a bit of the road surface home with me.

It's true I was childish. I wanted too much of everything; too much pleasure; my mouth opened to the world to kiss it and take it in. Children want to eat the world. It's a way of knowing. Touch the world. Stroke it, grasp it, pick it up, cram it into your mouth. Children who can't yet talk don't understand metaphor; they want mud; the real thing. As a child I made mud pies, sitting outside Dad's shed on his allotment. I watched him dig his vegetable plot; turning over the earth with his spade. Don't dig too deep, he said to me years later, when he realised I could talk: a spit's just right. One spit at a time, going from left to right; row after row; like writing. Worms like commas wriggled up and I gave them lifts in Dad's barrow. Sometimes I chopped the worms in half with Dad's spade to see if both halves still wriggled. I know it was cruel, but I like to know what things are made of and how they work. I prodded at my husband as I prodded earth and earthworms: let me love you; and he complained: don't dig too deep. Mud on my father's allotment held china and tin shards of memory, an agricultural past, and it held the repeated imprint of my thumb, the press of our Wellingtons. Now churchyard mud holds Dad, and Mum too. They're baked in a holy mud pie; beaks sticking up out of the mud crust, mud blackbirds still warbling hymns at me. They've rotted to good compost inside me. I fork them up from time to time. I turn them over gently. Like leaf mould. Like the leaves of a book.

I flicked over the leaves of my story so far, felt at a loss, determined to begin my story again, took the job in eastern England. Most mornings, all through that autumn and winter when I lived with the gentle widow, I left her house to walk in to work, rather than hitching a lift, and it rained. Fine drizzle wetted my face. The ploughed fields formed long ripples of mud, as though they were a beach abandoned by the retreating tide. The sky gleamed opal and pearl, and white mist like mohair threaded the thorny black hedgerows. I marched along the muddy side of the gravelled road, its surface broken and roughed up, following the length of the field; one field after another; a soft strobe of mud; my eyes levelling with the deep furrows, the turned, buttery earth. When the fog dispersed, the sun burst out: each clod sparkled, cast a tiny precise shadow; the field glittered, shapes of pale brown and purple and coffee and black broken up, gleaming like chocolate; tilted blocks that stretched far away; and a fringe of hairy elms on the horizon. I passed a pink-washed farm, a clump of cottages with kitchen gardens neat as Dad's, ruled with dotted lines of leeks. I studied the tall knobbed twists of turquoise Brussels sprouts; the pure pale green of cabbages, tight-waisted and frilly; about to bolt. (I'd bolted; donned my black suede shoes and run away.) Yes I could have eaten a handful of earth, dry-damp-delicious in my mouth, and I could have eaten the long woven hedges and the bright grass and the black thorns glossy as silver. I wanted to lick all of it, taste it and swallow it and be one with it. And then, dissolving, I wasn't myself, I wasn't myself any more. I'd gone. I was just part of the mud, fresh in the rain and the sun and I was fed by the world, mouth open, full, churning with joy.

At work, in the white university building beyond the great park, in the office attached to the campus gallery, I turned over words. I dug into language, I moulded lumps of it between my hands, it formed half moons under my fingernails. I picked at these earthy crescents until they broke into crumbs which I swept together until they formed sentences I could edit; the introduction to an exhibition catalogue. Outside, students and lecturers tapped from one concrete tower to the next. I studied the artist given the job of curating the show: his blue eyes, his big hands. He walked me round the gallery. I could look, I could touch, I could talk, as much as I wanted to. On some canvases, the work of a woman painter who cherished the texture of flesh, the oil paint creased so heavy and thick that when the paintings were first hung the paint began to slide off, down towards the floor, and the artist had to catch the loose body of the paintings in his hands; cradle it. Shrugs and ripples of paint like the ripples of mud in the field, the ripples of mud in the estuary when the tide slumped out.

Springtime inched and shivered in, pigeons and gulls twirling above the estuary in a grey metal sky. With the artist I went for a walk along the river. A bottle of red wine in his coat pocket and camembert sandwiches in mine. We lay on the muddy river bank, kissing, at three in the afternoon. We rolled each other over and over like cylindrical seals, we rolled our trousers down, we pressed each other into the mud, we imprinted our names our bodies, we stamped ourselves into each other into the mud then heard cries and laughter, a boat going past, two men leaning on their oars and shouting to the artist good on yer matey.

Before coming to this eastern county I'd been in a sad, a sorry state, like a mould split in two, broken open, but no precious casting inside. A mussel shell with no mussel. An oyster lacking a pearl. At night in my rented room I knocked, clumsy and speechless, between four plaster-board walls. My arms flailed empty, shaped to a body that had gone. Now on that chilly picnic on the riverbank I had earth in my mouth and that meant I was alive and I could taste mud and I mouthed to the artist and nibbled and licked him and we were each other's camembert red wine mud feast and we waved to the men gawping from their boat and blew them on their way with gales of laughter.

Hurricanes of laughter. We both remembered the hurricane a few months previously. I'd walked about in the park, watching the men inspecting the damage, tidying up with chain-saws. A heap of lopped trees, thrusting their maimed limbs forward. Amputations. Traumatic, like the end of a marriage. The chopped trunks of the fallen pines were blue; bracts of blue; black; pearl. People bunched together and peered down into the caverns of mud left by the uplifted roots. The hurricane had twisted through, stood the park on its head and then sped off. An honest, delinquent wind, enacting its rage, creating havoc, accepting no responsibility.

In March the scarred landscape furred with green, as soft and tender to touch as the suede of my shoes. I rode around the flat countryside on the back of the artist's motor-bike, exploring. He showed me his rented room, at the other end of the village from mine, and his temporary studio in the lean-to shed next door. At the moment he was making pots. I remembered Dad on his allotment, and the clay shells I'd made and given to him which he broke with one stomp of his Wellington boot.

The artist was making pots like little mud babies. Experiments. Some, the successes, he painted with slip and fired in a kiln and others, the failures, he took down to the estuary. He laid them flat on the sheeny mud and abandoned them to the tide; mud to mud.

I parked my black suede shoes at one side of the low double bed in his attic bedroom. I lifted them up, tapped them on the floor, knocked them until flakes of brown mud fell off the soles. I picked up the curls of mud and balanced them on my palms. Loops and half-circles of mud. Mud words. Mud commas and full stops. Bits of writing, broken apart, like the pieces of an old pot you dig up when going over your allotment. I'd piece them back together again, make something new with them.

Colette Looks Back

I was my mother's youngest child, her darling. I was her Rapunzel and she my tower. Her arms encircled me, swooped me up to bed at night, held me safe.

Every evening she unravelled my hair. Loosened, it reached my hips. She brushed it out. It sprang alive, crackling and flaring, and she struggled with it, subduing it, tugging at knots. I was a meadow of dried cut grass and she raked me up and I snapped back. Then she twisted the crisp mass into two thick plaits which lay docilely on my shoulders, ready for the night.

My mother called my long, rippling hair her treasure. But my hair was my own treasure first, and then Jean-Luc's. In the barn that day I held the tips of my plaits in my hands, stretched them out and embraced him. I tied him to me with my ropes of hair.

I'd followed him in to find the cat and her new kittens. Stacked golden bales loomed over us. White sunlight knifed in through the half-open door from the yard outside. Grain dust, soft underfoot, silted up the corners.

Fragrance of hay: sweet, almost fermenting. Heat pressed onto our shoulders, felled us. Down we dropped. High above us, the branching timbers of the roof. We lay on a bed of parched stalks covered with empty flour sacks. Coarse linen paler than his brown face, brown hands. I want to kiss you, I said. We were eleven years old. I'd never yet kissed a boy. He was the first.

The village school was just two streets away from my parents' house, near the church, on the far side of the market-place. Childhood meant wildness, going barefoot all summer if I wanted, freedom to roam the woods and fields on my own; tearing madly home at dusk after staying out too late. In the school yard, in between lessons, boys and girls played together. Once we turned ten years old, however, new rules issued up from nowhere and constricted us, separated us. We ran and swaggered in separate gangs, stuck to different games. Boys no longer joined in girls' elaborate hopscotch and skipping rituals. Girls who, a year before, had linked arms with boys, screaming and whooping, to play wars – a line of children swooping towards the opposite enemy line, determined to crash into it, crush it – were banned now from kicking balls about or leapfrogging over rows of bent backs. Girls whispered in groups by the black stove in the centre of the classroom. Boys hunted in packs outside.

I'd always been a tomboy. I didn't have to care about pleasing grown-ups. My father, the tax collector, accepted me as his fellow dreamer, his companion on trips in the horse and cart to outlying villages and farms. My mother, the goddess of the hearth, acknowledged my temporary freedoms, tolerated my scabbed knees and dirty face as long as she could grasp me between her knees at night and re-do my hair. My long plaits might fly out behind me when I ran pell-mell down the cobbled hill to our house, but to me they simply meant I was a runaway horse with reins trailing. I scowled rather than smiled when casually-met grown-ups chucked me under the chin and cooed at me. My black school overall was always ripped, inkstained, with buttons missing. My boots were always scuffed.

I wanted to remain a tomboy, not to have to grow up, turn into a mincing young lady with corsets and hair pieces and rouge pots; not to feel forced to compete with my friends. I felt girls begin to betray me, lining up for the prettiness-and-pleasing stakes. They frightened me too. They seemed like sleepwalkers. In turn I frightened them: they considered me too rough, and backed off. When I seized them by the hand and whirled them across the playground they'd fall over and start crying. I leaned against the wall, sulking, watching the others play. Part of me wanted to be like them, and so not to be excluded; that made me run faster and shout louder than ever. I heard them talking about me once: oh, she's weird, but not a bad sort, if only she didn't use such long words.

How could I help it if I loved reading? I loved my

father, and loved being near him. He let me into his study, let me read whatever I liked, and I worked my way through his complete library. Botany, geology, biology, I learned about them all; learned their vocabularies. Such precision, a kind of poetry, fascinated me. The tiniest part of something had its own distinct name. I learned this through living in the house, and also through living in my father's books. My mother named plants, animals, foodstuffs, implements, my father the stars and the layers of the earth. They named and separated things; that was how you knew things. You had to keep them apart. They weren't in charge of explaining girls, explaining boys. Those words didn't matter to me while I was still a girl-boy, a boygirl.

I noticed Jean-Luc because sometimes he too hung about on his own. How do you know what first attracts you? I'd known him all my life as one of the boys who came in to school from the farms outside the village. We learned our hierarchies early on: the sons of shopkeepers fought the sons of peasants, just as the girls from the village looked down on the girls from the outlying hamlets. Jean-Luc managed to keep a certain distance from these feuds. I began to see him as himself, not just part of a group who chased and tormented any girl crossing their path. He had a thin, bony face, brown as a hazelnut. Fair hair cropped short, hazel eyes, a beak of a nose. He was wiry, but not tall. I began to notice other things. How he used his nimble tongue to get out of trouble with the bullies but fought when he had to, fierce as any driven terrier worrying a rat. He could be funny. He had a way of cracking jokes quietly, laughing without making a sound, lips pressed together, laughing with just his eyes, his whole body shaking with mirth. I tried not to laugh, not to acknowledge I was listening to repartee directed only at boys, but I could tell he knew he had my attention.

He lived with his father and mother, on a farm two kilometres outside the village, a little way into the forest. Wild boar ran to and fro in its depths, emerging to trample and eat the young tips of crops. The men hunted them down, shared out the meat. The forest gave us chestnuts, and mushrooms, and bilberries. The deer trotted out of it, seeking water, and could be shot in season. In late winter we cut young birch branches there, dragged them home, sorted them into bundles that we tied with wire to make brooms. We picked up kindling from the sides of the paths. The forest provided for us: larder and playground; boundary. Beyond it lived people we didn't know. Another country. Beyond that: Paris.

One July afternoon, Jean-Luc arrived at my parents' house in the village main street with a wooden-topped basket containing two dead cockerels sent by his mother as a gift. Gifts knotted our little community together in a tight mesh of obligation and gratitude. Perhaps the gift had something to do with the fact that my father was the local tax collector. I didn't know. Jean-Luc flipped up the two centrally hinged lids of the basket to show us the contents. With my mother I inspected the two red combs, the glossy feathers, the limp, gnarled legs, the bunched claws. Jean-Luc said, in response to my mother's questioning, that he had killed the cockerels himself. In our household it was my mother who slaughtered the poultry, hanging them up by their trussed feet from a hook on the back of the shed door and then slitting their throats with the knife she kept in the pocket of her apron.

Wait, my mother said: let me find some pots of preserves for you to take back with you.

She vanished up the outside steps to the grenier, the granary turned store-room, where all such things were kept, and Jean-Luc and I stood in the back garden at the top of the flight of stone steps that led down to the flowerbeds and vegetable plot.

I studied him. How clean he looked. Scrubbed up for this visit, as though he were off to Mass or catechism class. Ironed blue shirt and blue trousers. Well-blacked boots. Suddenly my arms wanted to open, take him in as knowledge: he was part of the gift. His mother had sent him to me.

I pestered him with questions. He told me that yes, he knew how to handle a gun, how to kill and skin a rabbit. He'd helped his father with the lambing, had watched cows give birth.

Our cat's just had kittens, he said.

My mother stepped rapidly down the wooden staircase from the grenier, heels clacking. She held out two earthenware jars of redcurrant jam. She didn't want to be too beholden for the gift of the cockerels and so she wished to send something back in exchange. Presents worked like that. They went back and forth instead of money.

My mother sent me off with Jean-Luc, the basket and the pots of jam. Her arms closed against us, her hands clapped and she shooed us away. I was my mother's treasure and she was giving me to Jean-Luc.

Remember, you're to be back well before it's dark, she instructed me. Remember your manners.

We went the long way round to his farm. In order not to waste time we should have gone direct. We should have taken the main road between the fields where everybody was out harvesting, but we chose the back route: more interesting and more private. In fact there was so much to see that ours turned into the very longest way possible, rambling and roundabout with plenty of stops. I encouraged these. I didn't want our walk to end. Mindful of how girls were supposed to behave, I pretended the opposite. Fiddling my fingers over the cool twist of the basket's handle, I tried to sound indifferent whenever I spoke to him.

We turned off the path by mute consent and plunged through a thicket of cow-parsley down towards the stream that ran between banks of wild mint.

Won't you get into trouble for dawdling? I asked:

your mother must have been expecting you sooner than this.

We were stabbing sticks through the green scum of water weeds clogging the edges of the lazy stream. Crouching next to him I felt the sun strike, scorch, burnish the back of my neck. It burnished him too. The sun made us equal, as did the fact that we were the same height. Both of us skinny and sturdy. Both able to run fast, whistle, and use our fists.

He shrugged.

I don't care.

We had made our way through the leafy tunnels that formed the lanes linking meadows, the hedgerows growing so high that their tops met overhead. Every spring they were cut back to keep the path clear for moving herds of cows between pastures, and every midsummer they sprouted full and thick with greenery again. They would become overgrown in a single season if allowed to grow unchecked, like the briar hedge swallowing up Sleeping Beauty's palace. Swinging the basket, bumping it rhythmically against my thigh, I liked the feeling of dissolving into all that green. We picked bunches of coarse weeds and whipped each other's bare legs with them, then bandaged each other with dock leaves. We held buttercups under each other's chins, tickled each other's wrists with thorny twigs, tied our feet together with laces of vetch and tried to run three-legged. Horse flies wove buzzing clouds above our heads and we had to slap them away. I smelled cattle, and cowpats, and wild garlic in the ditches, and hot grass, and him, very close to me as we dawdled along the rutted track, our elbows brushing. He smelled of carbolic soap, and of his own sweat breaking through. Fresh sweat's a good smell. Like on horses. I snuffed it up.

Finally we reached a path that skirted the forest on one side and had fields full of grazing sheep on the other. We pushed through the rusted iron gate and into the yard. The dog barked and bounded up to greet us. His mother, summoned by the dog's joy, came out of the kitchen. Heat stained her face red. Escaped strands of scraped back hair caught under a plain white cap looked lank and wet. She wore a faded blue-checked dress with a grey pinafore over it.

Where have you been!

I could tell she felt she had to be more polite to me than she wanted; as a result she spared Jean-Luc a scolding. She took back her basket, studied the jars of redcurrant jam in it, thanked me unsmilingly.

I'll bring the jars back to your mother once they're empty, she said.

So it would go on. Back and forth. Back and forth.

Jean-Luc's mother was a tall, thin woman, with deepset blue eyes. A faded blue, like the colour of her dress, like the pattern on old plates after many washings. She wore her sleeves rolled to the elbow, hooked back with pins. Her arms were wiry and muscled as a man's.

How strong she seemed. My mother was strong too, but she hid it under bustles and trailing skirts. This woman, standing legs apart, feet planted in clogs, looked tough enough for anything. I glanced at her big hands, her floury knuckles, her short fingernails crusted with dough. If you tried to get near those kneading hands you'd be clouted away. Mind my pastry! Whereas my mother's hands captured me, caressed me, knew me, clenched me close, didn't let me go.

Say thank you to your mother.

She nodded dismissal, stalked off towards her kitchen. I looked at her back, the determined set of her shoulders.

Jean-Luc was due to bring the cows in for milking a little later on, but first of all he took me all around the farm. Deserted: his father and brothers were out working on the harvest. He'd been let off to come over to my house, but tomorrow he'd have to work extra hard to make up for it. Patiently he showed me everything I wanted to see: the donkey, the pony, the hens and ducks, the sheep. Patiently he explained what everything was for: the harnesses, the tools, the tubs and buckets.

We circled back to the yard and went into the hot, dark barn. No cat and kittens visible. Cats moved their kittens from time to time, to keep them safe, I knew that. Picked them up, one by one, by the scruff of their necks, shifted them to new hiding-places.

Let's play horses, I proposed.

Jean-Luc seized the ends of my plaits as reins. I galloped,

neighing, around the central space inside the toppling bales of hay, pulling him after me. Then I turned round, and snared him. I stretched out my hands, holding the tips of my long plaits, and caught him. I tied him to me with my ropes of hair.

We sank down together, winded. Under our different clothes, under our skins, we were alike, that was what I felt, we were kin, we belonged together, and so it was natural first to hesitate and then to lean closer, to say: I want to kiss you. I touched my mouth to his. Immediately he gripped me and kissed me back.

Later on his mother screamed for him and he went off to fetch in the cows and I walked home. I helped my mother pluck and draw the cockerels, pull out the gooey red mess of their insides.

Jean-Luc and I played together all through that summer, whenever he could skive off his various jobs around the farm. On those occasions his mother spotted me, she tolerated me frowningly. Watched me with a suspicious eye. He and I kept out of her way as much as possible. We climbed trees, made dens in the hedges, set traps for mice and rats, fished in the stream, explored the tumbledown sheds behind the farmyard. He showed me the disused cottage at the edge of the property, where his grandparents had first lived, before they built the farmhouse. The forest towered over it. It seemed to me like a fallen tree-house, surrounded by a beech hedge, dandled among greenery, nettles and brambles twining it into themselves. Soon it would fall into complete disrepair. I wanted to make it go the other way: I wanted to mend it. I wanted to change it into a house people could live in again. I didn't like seeing it turn to rack and ruin.

Every so often we ended up in the barn. I learned him, like a geography lesson at school. I recited him, like tables. I spelled him out, tracing him with my finger. We learned each other: speechless, mouth on mouth, arms round each other, legs wound together. Then at length I'd sit up, drowsy with heat and kisses, smoothe myself down, race across the yard, run home along the forest path.

Late one afternoon, when I'd spent too long at the farm, when Jean-Luc should have been helping his brother muck out the cowshed, his mother came searching for the truant, caught us hugging each other on our bed of straw. A clip round the head for him, a cold shoulder turned on me. Scolding furiously, she drove him towards the house.

My mother frowned at my flushed face.

Where have you been? What have you been up to?

Nothing, I said.

I glowered.

What a mess you're in, she said: your hair's all undone and full of bits of hay.

She pulled me onto her lap and began unbraiding my plaits. She smacked the brush through my tangles. Little wretch, little tearaway, little rebel, oh my bad girl, my precious one, my treasure.

After that, Jean-Luc and I made the tumbledown cottage our hiding-place. The forest held us, all summer long, until autumn arrived.

Years passed. Once we both left school I hardly ever saw Jean-Luc. I went on knowing him: my hands knew him and so did my mouth. My skin still knew him. My plaits remembered how they had twirled round him and captured him. Did he remember me? I didn't know. I knew he was going to get married to a local girl and bring his bride home to his parents' house. I glimpsed his fiancée at market one day, when I accompanied my mother there to help her with the shopping. My mother casually pointed her out, standing next to a big basket of eggs. She wasn't anyone I remembered from school. The spitting image of his mother she seemed to me: tall, slender, fair hair pulled back in a bun, neat feet in polished clogs. I saw her glance at my young lady's get-up: smart serge skirt, sailor blouse, beret with a rosette. She's called Agathe, my mother said, noticing me looking. A saint's name sounding like agate; hard and burnished as a jewel. Jean-Luc chose her as his jewel. I thought that perhaps I remained the secret pebble he carried in his pocket; a souvenir. Jewel in one pocket; pebble in another.

Before I was twenty years old I became engaged to Willy. Stout, moustachioed, licentious, Parisian Willy, the journalist, the entrepreneur who kept a factory of impoverished literary hacks churning out the novelettes that made his fortune. Willy, who was my escape route from my adored, all-possessing, country-goddess mother.

Willy of course believed, given my youth, that I remained an innocent little savage, that my family delivered me up to him as a virgin sacrifice, that I'd never seen a naked man before and certainly not one with an erection. On our wedding night he'd be the teacher and I his docile pupil. I'd prance for him on the stage of our bed, watch my shadow tremble on the wall, watch my dark shape waver as the shadow of his huge cock loomed up beside me. Oh oh oh! Oh la la! Blah blah blah and so on and so forth.

I was due to get married in late autumn. First of all I had to get ready. All through September I hemmed my new petticoats and chemises, my new sheets. October: season of picking, bottling, preserving. In my mother's garden the cherry tree leaves turned golden, pink, orange. Red fruits studded the apple trees. We shook them down onto canvas sheets. In the mornings spiderswebs, beaded with brilliant dewdrops, laced the hedges, the scarlet points of rosehips and haws.

Then the weather changed. Often now it rained, long sweeping showers of grey, and the mists wrapped themselves around the house and crept along the village street. The sun appeared only at mid-day, glimmering pale gold, and then vanished again. October melted into November, the coming of winter.

Four days before my wedding to Willy I sent a message

to Jean-Luc, entrusting it to one of the village children, bribing him with a bag of macaroons. Two days before my marriage, I told my mother one afternoon I needed a walk, then slipped out when she wasn't looking, so that she couldn't point out that it was raining, and didn't see what direction I took.

Wrapped in my father's big coat, a big cap hiding my face and hair, I went towards the forest. I made for the farm, for the disused cottage where Jean-Luc waited for me. I squelched over mud, over mashed leaves. Once I entered the forest, greyness muffled the world. Fog hung under the trees. I stepped carefully: I could hardly see a metre ahead. The world shrunk to impenetrable grey mist. On either side of the deep rutted track enormous toadstools sprouted, red ones with white spots, luminous blue-mauve ones, fluted like trumpets. The air, steeped in moisture, put clammy hands to my face. I smelled wet earth, wet leaf-mould. Such silence! Inside it I heard tiny sounds. I heard rain dropping. Pattering on leaves, on fallen logs. No birds. A veil of silence: no light. The thick mist banished the afternoon; made night come early. I stumbled and slid on the narrow path clogged with fallen leaves on top of soft mud; unstable and very slippery.

I turned into the lane that led to the cottage. Into a tunnel of darkness I plunged, tree branches meeting overhead, rain soaking my shoulders through my coat. The light of a lantern shone through the darkness. I trod through the opening in the beech hedge. The forest loomed above me like a circle of wolves with open mouths. I fumbled with the latch. The wet stone wall felt solid with cold. I pushed the door open and went in.

The cottage smelled of damp. At first we kept our coats on. He wore a big coat, a bit too big for him, green and felted as the covering of walnuts you gather early for pickling. Water streamed from our coats onto the mud floor. He lit a fire with kindling and branches he told me he'd brought across the day before. In front of the fire he made us a bed with ferns he'd cut and stacked to dry. A thick mattress of springy ferns smelling of greenness, and some clean linen sacks laid on top. The fire roared up and chased away the cold. Nobody will see the smoke through the mist, he said: we're safe.

Years later I'd write my girly porno for Willy, about my childhood in the village, the goings-on at school. I'd fake it, to please him, I'd work up salacious details, to titillate him, earn my pin-money. Whereas with Jean-Luc it wasn't like that at all.

At first I told myself I just wanted to say goodbye. Years, perhaps, before I'd see him again. He looked exactly the same. Brown and complete as a hazelnut. We blurted out a few bits of nonsense. Circled each other, keeping plenty of space between us. Then I screwed up my courage and went closer. His smell hadn't changed.

I want to kiss you, I said.

I leaned towards him. Meaning, I think, to give him just a swift kiss. Whatever I intended didn't matter.

Immediately, he seized me. His wide, light tongue filled my mouth. My hands flew up. I pulled off my cap, shook and loosened my plaits. I tore them apart with my fingers. I unravelled my hair and wrapped it around us. Covered by my streams of hair we sank down onto our makeshift bed. We knew each other so well: no fumbling and no fuss. His cock felt dry and warm. It swung up between my hands. I pulled him into me as he pushed inside me. We played a new game of animals who could speak, we made a new animal between us. Warmth concentrated and rose inside me, slowly bloomed like a gold flower.

He walked me back to the edge of the forest and I squelched home. Wedding nerves, such nonsense, darling, scolded my mother: you could have caught your death of cold. She ripped off my sodden coat, my blouse and skirt, stripped off my soaked muddy stockings, towelled me dry. She tutted over the blood on my petticoat: so that's what the matter is, you've got your period, that's all.

The road ahead divided: the road I took and the road I didn't. If I'd married Jean-Luc, become a farmer's wife, borne his children, stayed all my life in one place, would I ever have had other adventures? In any event, he didn't ask me. He said goodbye to me and I to him.

I went ahead and married Willy and with him I boarded the train for Paris and very soon afterwards I cut my hair.

Vegetarian in France

It was not easy, being a vegetarian in France.

Larry could just about manage in Paris and other large cities, but in rural society he was done for. On their holidays he and Nicolette stuck to picnics. At lunchtime you could turn off down a lane and park near a river or at the entrance to a forest, get out the folding table and chairs, and enjoy your camembert, baguette and tomatoes with no one looking at you and criticising. Harder in the evening, though, when he wanted both to avoid the mosquitoes and to eat something hot; almost impossible to find places willing to serve him the right food. Often enough Nicolette was forced to smuggle their little camping stove and cooking pots into their hotel bedroom and rustle him up some clandestine spaghetti, rather than face the incomprehension of the patronne in the restaurant downstairs. French country people, in particular the middle-aged and elderly ones, had no concept of not eating flesh. Animals existed and were raised to be killed and eaten and that was that.

It's not that I want to argue about it, Larry said: I just want something to eat. The French are so intolerant of anything different.

Oh darling, Nicolette said: it's just not in their culture, that's all.

When they drove south in the summer, Nicolette was sometimes able to persuade Larry to stop for lunch at a routier cafe. She liked the masculine ambiance, the atmosphere of cigarette smoke and the sports news blaring on TV and the long tables lined with hungry lorry drivers. She liked all the men looking at her as she walked in. French men really noticed women. However much they were concentrating on their bifteck and frites, they lifted an eye and appraised her face and frock and legs while she bobbed her head and murmured *Bonjour messieurs.* Then as the meal progressed she would peep at them sideways and eavesdrop on their conversations and smile shyly if they caught her eye.

The hors d'oeuvres presented no obstacle. You helped yourself from the array of cold dishes on the buffet. While Nicolette inspected the homemade rabbit pâté, the rillettes and saucisson and soused fillet of mackerel, before settling on a plateful of crudités so that she didn't look too greedy, Harry would pick out some olives, gherkins and hard-boiled eggs (he ate eggs, as he ate butter, cream and cheese – to hell with rennet being made from animals) and some sliced tomatoes, or perhaps some grated celeriac in mayonnaise.

With the main course came the real problem. While the routiers, and indeed Nicolette, were served the hot, delicious plat du jour, featuring pork, beef, lamb, chicken or veal, the most that Larry would ever be offered, once his eating requirements were explained, was an omelette. Even in quite posh restaurants, or perhaps especially in quite posh restaurants, harassed waiters and patronnes had little time for Nicolette's super-polite requests that her husband be given something described neither on the menu du jour nor on the carte. A blank look and much sighing would, if Larry were lucky, eventually be followed by the offer of an omelette.

Larry graded these omelettes on a scale of one to ten. Some came in at eight, plump and creamy and rolling in melted butter, with thin slices of mushrooms inside and a sprinkling of finely minced parsley on top. Some came in at nought: those incorporating cubes of bacon – someone in the kitchen trying to jazz things up or just be kind to the poor benighted Englishman – and which then had to be sent back.

Sometimes, if Larry was very fortunate indeed, the waiter would become inspired and suggest a plate of steamed vegetables before or after the omelette. Larry knew he should look grateful. Nicolette would smile sympathetically. Out of solidarity with him she would forswear calf's liver and onions, or sausages and lentils, or sweetbreads, or pork simmered with cream and apples and calvados; she would compromise and order fish, usually poached salmon or trout. Nothing with legs and nothing still with its face on, with eyes that looked at you. The waiters would shake their heads over the pair of them and slap down the carafe of wine and the basket of bread with contempt.

Nicolette was sure it was contempt. She was very sensitive to what other people thought of her and hated upsetting or offending anyone. She yearned to fit in and not attract criticism. For this reason, for example, she always dressed correctly. She felt ashamed of British tourists who loafed around foreign cities in beachwear, skimpy vests and shorts in shrieking colours, with too much red sunburned flesh on view. She wished that Larry would wear shoes rather than trainers. She herself favoured sandals, and neat linen skirts and blouses that went well with her pink cheeks and short blonde hair. People appraising her could recognise her as an Englishwoman but realise that she had made an effort. Similarly, despising those same tourists who expected everyone else to speak English, Nicolette had gone to French language evening classes for some years and was now quite proficient.

Larry liked French wine and the French climate and the French way of life (mainly) but claimed he had no ear for languages. What he actually had was a built-in resistance to learning anything he didn't see the point of. Important things came naturally and spontaneously. Sex, for example. You didn't have to learn that, did you? Nicolette had the gift of the gab and good luck to her. So it was Nicolette who, sitting down and shaking out her napkin, would smile sweetly and address the waiters in her best French, very formal and correct, with much deployment of please and thank you, but it was no use, once the moment of ordering the food arrived and she had once more to go through the rigmarole of pleading that Larry be given something he could actually eat, she would become flustered and anxious and begin trying to use the imperfect subjunctive and then flounder and stammer and start blushing, and the waiter would look first baffled, then impatient, and finally irritated and contemptuous. The patronne, that busy goddess circulating the dining-room, making sure that everything was going smoothly, would be summoned, and would courteously enquire what was the matter.

Nicolette eventually learned never to utter the word vegetarian. Instead she would say timidly: I am afraid my husband cannot eat meat or fish. He is unable to.

Madame la patronne would assume that some digestive or gastric disorder, probably located in that venerable organ the liver, was at issue, and would briskly announce: so why not an omelette? Or a plate of some steamed vegetables? And continue on her tour of the tables. People's eyes would swivel; they would stare at the mad English. Nicolette would feel their eyes boring scornfully into her back. She would bend her head humbly over her sliver of unadorned trout and eat it as unobtrusively as possible.

Matters improved once Larry retired at sixty-five and

he and Nicolette made the big decision to move to France full-time, because now Nicolette could cook Larry's favourite dishes at home. Many of these were in fact French classics. Onion tart, for instance, or leek and potato soup, or slices of potato layered in cream, or stuffed pancakes, or asparagus soufflé, or ratatouille. These were, obviously, also, vegetarian dishes. It was just that in French people's presence you hadn't to call them that.

They settled in the Dordogne, buying a cottage with just enough land to create a manageable garden. Nicolette planted vegetables and soft fruit, apple and cherry trees, a vine, all kinds of herbs. Larry sent round-robin emails to all the folks back home: we're living our dream. He enjoyed nothing more than sitting on the bench outside the front door watching the sunset with a glass of beer in his hand, while in the kitchen Nicolette shelled peas and beans for supper.

Nicolette felt restless but tried not to show it. She missed her teaching job. I'm only fifty-five, she said to her reflection in the bathroom mirror: that's not old, is it? She couldn't cook and clean all day long but what else was there to do? She settled for weekly dancing classes in the village hall, and also gardened ferociously. She pruned and lopped and chopped. She supervised the workmen who came in to do repairs. Such sweeties they were, the electrician and the carpenter and the plumber. So appreciative of the aperitifs she offered them. At village fetes they whirled her round the floor and complimented her on how well she danced.

The neighbours in the farm up the road, Monsieur and Madame Bonnefoi, invited Larry and Nicolette in for a drink one evening, then pressed them to stay for dinner. Nicolette felt obliged to refuse and to explain why.

But what would happen to all the animals if we didn't kill and eat them? exclaimed Monsieur Bonnefoi: there would be far too many of them, don't you see?

Nicolette geared herself up once more to rehearse Larry's pacifism towards dumb beasts, his love of nature and his respect for the ecological movement. In the light of the havoc caused by intensive farming methods, dubious supermarket practices, BSE, and the outbreak of foot and mouth disease, surely that made sense?

She swigged her sweet vermouth. She didn't like it much, but it was what her hostess was drinking. Women here, she had learned, were not supposed to ask for pastis or whisky.

Larry just prefers vegetables, she said.

The neighbours smiled.

Ah, he is a herbivore!

They were pleased with themselves. They shrugged their shoulders and exchanged significant looks. Nicolette had seen that shrug many times before. It said: what kind of a man is this? Can he really be called a man at all if he doesn't eat meat?

Larry sprawled in his chair, oblivious. Madame

Bonnefoi had set out an array of little savoury treats to accompany their drinks. Larry had necessarily refused the bits of crackling, the cocktail sausages, the bacon-flavoured mini-biscuits, but had accepted a second whisky with alacrity. Now he was full of edgy bonhomie, bored, wanting to be off home, not listening to anything anybody said because he couldn't understand it, but nonetheless instructing Nicolette to translate for him as soon as he had something to say.

She gave him a rapidly whispered version of the conversation so far. Larry interrupted her.

Hang on, old girl. Let me say something for once. Just tell them that being a vegetarian is brilliant for your sex life, right?

He punched the air with his empty glass. Nicolette laughed shrilly. She translated what he'd said. The Bonnefois roared with delight and toasted their new English neighbours afresh. Monsieur Bonnefoi slapped Larry on the back and told Nicolette how lucky she was.

Larry discouraged Nicolette from accepting any other dinner invitations, because it was so boring for him having to sit there all evening in silence while everyone talked in French, having to prod Nicolette to say for him whatever he wanted to say. So Nicolette visited her new neighbours in the daytime. She and Madame Bonnefoi made friends. To cement their friendship, they regularly exchanged small gifts. Nicolette gave Madame Bonnefoi bunches of flowers and herbs from her garden, and

Madame Bonnefoi gave Nicolette a couple of trout from the lake, still twitching and thrashing in their plastic bag, a pot of goose fat, and some duck's blood for making boudin. She let Nicolette watch the pig being slung up by the hind legs from the forklift truck to be butchered, and showed her how you scoured off the bristles with a blow-torch. She showed her how to kill and gut poultry, and demonstrated various methods of skinning rabbits once you'd broken their necks. One way was to gouge out the eyes, take a knife to the sockets, and peel the skin off from there. In a few minutes the fluffy white fur was tugged away and the naked head and body were filmed with rapidly seeping red.

Sometimes, on frosty winter mornings, Nicolette heard the hunt go by, the yapping of the excited dogs as they poured across the rigid silver of the bare, furrowed fields, the exultant repeated call of the hunters' horns. Wrapping herself in her quilted jacket, she would hurry to the open door and strain her eyes against the sparkling light for a view of the escaping prey. The hunters wore olive-green coats and sturdy boots. They waved to her from where they stood in the lane, gossiping, guns crooked over their arms. Monsieur Bonnefoi would bring home his share of the dead beast, and Nicolette would watch his wife cut it up and parcel it for the freezer. Boars had to be culled, Madame Bonnefoi instructed her, because they savaged the crops and spoilt everything. They had to be put down.

Larry was found murdered one afternoon in January, his throat expertly slit from ear to ear. The gendarmes asked Nicolette whether her husband had had any enemies, and she replied that, as a vegetarian, he had certainly found it difficult to fit in.

Emma Bovary's Ghost

That woman called Emma Bovary died, but the girl who was Emma before she got married lives on. She surprises me, jumping out of silence and darkness, a shiver across my skin, she jumps up inside me and talks to me. I stay as still as possible, trying not to frighten her away. She goes on telling me her story. Don't stop, I beg her: don't stop.

Stories are hard to get a hold on. They change like shadows on a day of sun and wind. They flicker like candles in draughts in the evening. If you don't pay them enough attention they dwindle and die, black wicks smoking above puddles of wax.

Sometimes one story hides inside another, like a handkerchief lost inside the folds of a white nightdress laid on top of a pile of ironing. Sometimes one story falls out of another, the nightdress picked up and shaken and dropped over the back of a chair and the handkerchief floating, half-remembered, down to the floor.

The stories of our childhood, Emma's and mine, are as

real and as flimsy as ghosts. Emma's ghost dances above me, at the top of the stairs, a small girl in a blue linen dress hopping from foot to foot, laughing, then leaning over the banister to call down to me. Come and play sultans and slaves. Come and play knights and damsels. Come and play troubadours. Then she vanishes.

I've thought a lot about ghosts. Usually when you see one in daylight you don't know it's a ghost. You think it's a person, fully alive. Just a stranger you've not met before, or someone you know well whom you don't know is dead. You find out afterwards. You look back, and you work out what's been going on. Something odd about the encounter nudges you, some strange detail, and then you meet someone who tells you the person's story and that they're dead, and so then you realise you met a ghost. Probably lots of people see ghosts but just don't realise. In the village where I grew up people saw ghosts all the time. Quite normal. Sometimes by day and sometimes by night. Often they came to warn you; to tick you off.

Emma started off as we all do: alive not dead, not a ghost, but flesh and blood. I first noticed her in catechism class in the village church, when we were both nine years old. Of course I knew who she was. We'd grown up in the same village. Her family, with their own farm, looked down on mine, who had no land. We were just peasants working for other people. That day our group of little girls sat in front of the side altar on low chairs with scratchy straw seats and the curé droned us through questions and answers on the love of God, the difference between body and soul. When Emma stood up to recite the Hail Mary, I suddenly found myself studying her as though I'd never seen her before: her black ringlets and dark eyes, her blue overall, her little feet planted in sturdy sabots. Her rosy lips pouting over the Latin words. Sunlight poured through the stained-glass window at her side and painted her head and shoulders scarlet and purple and gold. At that moment I fell for her.

I invented her. That's what falling in love means. You make the person into your own special beloved. You think you know the person but you don't. You see her as though she were a stranger. The same as seeing ghosts. Go towards them, touch them, and they dissolve and you're left with just a stripe of lamplight lying across the backs of your hands like the weal raised by a whip.

Emma is a story and a ghost and I loved her and she haunts me still. She hurt me. That was one of her favourite games once we had made friends: to pick up her whip and tickle me with it. She mounted me and I carried her round the farm garden; I was her faithful steed and I galloped along the gravel paths and she whipped me to make me go faster. Once I turned sixteen her father noticed my strong arms and employed me as a servant, to cook their meals and do their washing.

Charles Bovary didn't notice me when he came into

the farm kitchen that first time. For him I was transparent as air. I did not exist. He didn't believe in ghosts. I was the ghost he never knew haunted him and stalked her. How could I tell her I loved her? She'd only have laughed or looked disgusted. She'd have pushed me away. Charles didn't see me because I was the maid doing the ironing, and he was too busy staring at black-haired Emma, so smart in her blue merino dress with its three flounces round the hem, her dainty canvas boots. With my back to them, I sweated over my iron. Over my shoulder I peeped at him: his small blue eyes, his thick fingers clutching his hat, his mouth falling open as he gaped at Emma.

Her trick: not to speak a single word, for five minutes at least, just to glide to and fro, languidly picking up the pitcher, setting the cider cups onto the tray, pouring out the cider, so that he had time to appreciate her slender waist, her neat ankles and wrists, her long fingers with their delicate oval nails. She'd been away to convent school. The nuns had got good hold of her, combed and brushed and smoothed her wildness into place, taught her to be a lady. Charles was done for. He'd never seen anything like it: the sidelong glance with which she offered him a slice of buttered honeycake, the sweet curve of her lips as she offered to re-fill his cider cup. I was no different to Charles. I was done for too.

As he was leaving, she found his whip for him, where he'd dropped it behind the door. She handed him the whip. He blushed. She looked at him directly and smiled. He didn't know why but I did: she'd mastered him.

She'd had plenty of practice on me. When she returned from the convent, with a trunk full of watercolours and albums and keepsakes, she needed an audience to appreciate her new talents for playing the piano, doing embroidery, reciting long poems with all the correct theatrical gestures. She chose me. She'd get me to come into her bedroom and turn out the cupboard, re-folding her nightdresses and chemises and kerchiefs, putting them in neat heaps on the bed, tacking new strips of paper lace to the edges of the shelves. While I worked she'd tell me the stories of the novels she loved to read, stories of romance and adventure, and make me help her act them out. Sometimes I played the man and sometimes she did. We took turns to be the one who offered the first kiss, the one who demanded embraces, the one who snatched them. With flashing eyes she would stamp her booted feet and twirl her imaginary moustaches and wave her sword while I shrank back against the snowy pile of underclothes and pretended to be afraid.

She took me with her when she married Charles and left the village where she'd grown up and been so bored. Through the half-open kitchen door I heard her explain to him: Félicité's too plain and too poor ever to marry. She can be my maid.

She hoped for great things from the change in her life, but quite quickly she discovered she didn't much like the new house and the new village and the new husband. Charles wouldn't behave as she wanted him to. He didn't understand the games she wanted him to play.

One night, coming back into the salon, after I'd cleared away the supper dishes and washed up, to see if they wanted me to fetch more wood for the fire, I caught her trying to explain to him. Look. This is how you should hold yourself. This is how you should walk. She drew herself up, shoulders back, chin out. She tossed her head. She waved her hand. He slouched near the mantelpiece, then reached up for his tobacco tin. He moved like an old man. A good round belly he had on him too. He was starting to coarsen and to get fat and it irritated her. Now she spotted his whip that he'd thrown down on a chair, seized it and brandished it. Don't play with that inside the house, he said: you might hurt yourself. She shrugged and dropped it. Now between forefinger and thumb she flourished an imaginary cigar. What on earth are you playing at? he asked. She propped one little booted foot on the seat of her armchair, leaned forward, elbow on thigh. She was being The Man, just as we'd played together, she was showing him what to do, but Charles just gawped at her, a daft grin on his red face, as she brought her foot back down to the floor, stamped it, picked up the whip again and twirled it over her head. Finally he got the message, lurched towards her, hands out. Neither of them paid me any attention, though I was sure she at least knew I was there. I shut the door on them and retired to my room in the attic and left them to it. Their bedroom was just below mine. Soon I heard them come upstairs. Their bed creaked gently for a bit, then more forcefully, once twice thrice, and then the bed was obviously exhausted and fell asleep and then the bed snored.

Sometimes she came into the kitchen to complain to me, but not often. Now she was a married lady she was even higher above me than she'd been before. She'd have lost face with her neighbours if they'd known she confided in her servant. Silently I listened to her grumbles, and carried on with the task of the moment: stringing beans, scouring pots, cleaning shoes and boots, mixing starch, plunging my iron into the frills and folds of her nightgowns and nightcaps and drawers. She no longer touched me or invited me to play with her. She took lovers. Of course she did. She had the best of excuses: her husband gave her little pleasure and so she sought it elsewhere. Her boots, the canvas soaked and stained, told me their story. They didn't get that clotted with mud from just mincing round the garden. Those boots ran her down the lanes at evening to trysts in the forest. She gave me the boots, pair by pair as she muddied them, as a bribe.

I kept my mouth shut for a while. I watched her grow more desperate, more hectic, more careless. One summer afternoon, when she came in flushed, swinging her bonnet in one hand, her fichu open because of the heat, I warned her: be careful. She screamed at me: mind your insolence. She turned me out.

I didn't want to return to the village in which she and I had grown up. I moved twenty kilometres away, to Rouen, where there were other women like me. I found companions. By day I worked in a factory and at night I went to the bar and drank and smoked and sometimes danced. In the city I lost myself and became someone else and forgot all about Emma, her great black eyes, her black hair tumbling down her back to her waist when I pulled out her hairpins, her little white feet I held in my hands, the way she'd lie back with her hands demurely crossed on her white breast. Oh yes I forgot all about her I tell you, I buried her deep in my mind under layers of whiteness and she only emerged at night when I slept and could not be in control of my dreams. Once I met her at the mid-Lent carnival ball. To come in to Rouen and not be recognised she wore a half-mask, and she'd dressed up in a man's curled wig, a dark frock-coat with gold lacing, a pair of black breeches, and red stockings. My sweet tomboy, whistling and twirling her whip and brandishing her cigar. I started to laugh. She approached me and bowed: may I have the honour of this dance? I shook out my skirts and curtseyed and flirted my fan: yes, certainly. Away we went, twirling around the hall to the music of the brass band, and it was heaven to be in her arms again; to feel her soft skin, her cheek against my shoulder, her mouth so close to mine; we danced together all night and then at dawn she had to leave me to go back to her husband and I woke up shivering because my coverlet had slipped off as I slept.

How can she possibly be dead? She still comes to me, on Sunday nights as I sit by the fire, and she's not a ghost, she's alive, we are girls together again making up stories and we are full of hope.

Flâneuse

Summer evening. Polly puts on her red sleeveless dress. She comes out bare-legged, wanting to feel the air stroke her; brush her calves. Even this chilly weather brings sensual pleasure: her skin, warm from the indoors, smoothed by coolness. She walks through Southwark under grey skies, through fine rain which wets her bare feet sliding in jewelled leather flip-flops. New, bought this morning, they speed her along like Mercury's winged sandals. To do them justice she has painted her toenails a shimmery pale green, but now those little shields of pearl turn brown. Mud seeps and flurries up from the pavement. Little curds of mud plug the gaps between her toes; they'll crack and dry there once she gets inside; brown crescents, brown tidemarks on her skin. For now, liquid mud outlines her feet, as she sees when she glances down. Mud edges her toe tips, her toenails, like a stumpy soft-tipped pencil making a drawing. Tiny raindrops throw a net of moisture over her hair; she puts up her fingers and touches it. She imagines the sparkle of these tiny crystalline beads of rain; still just separate; like images in a dream you connect in the morning, webbing them into a narrative, a story.

She shakes her head and pearls of water fly round her face. Her feet slither in her damp flip-flops as she descends the slope from London Bridge Station, trains rumbling and shuddering overhead. The passages around Borough Market smell of exhaust fumes, refuse, rotting flowers. The pavement slabs rear and tilt; small ramps for sliding rain.

She flows along with the early evening crowd. The river of people rushing through the streets reveals pattern and connection, like networks of inky lines pushing through white pages, filling them, like blood coursing through veins. The city is a body, its heart pumping the people through, and she pulses along with all the others, part of them, separate from them, anonymous and yet herself. She chooses a backstreet route so that she crosses over into the unknown. She plunges down dingy alleys, gets lost, finds her bearings again. Gazes at glossy buildings she's never seen before, newly arisen since last month on the ruined sites of old office blocks, studies details of façades and posters and graffiti, old brick walls, crumbling stucco-covered pilasters, fragment of mosaic pavement, the portals of Victorian pubs.

At St Paul's a sudden squall of rain drives her into the tube. Puddles on the concrete steps down. The stuffy ticket hall pulses with sweat and damp clothes. Passengers hustle onto the platform. People going out for Friday night. All done up, glittering with the promise of cocktails, dancing. She breathes them in, their flowery perfume and spicy aftershave. The smells catch her throat; chokingly; she wants to cough.

She alights at Embankment. Flurry of pink and crimson clouds. The rain cleared away, the air fresh and cool, patches of damp smudge the grey pavements. She plunges into blue dusk. Along the Strand, up east of Trafalgar Square to St Martin's Lane and the Coliseum.

She wriggles into the mirrored foyer through the press of patrons, looks about for William's tall figure, big-nosed profile. She shrugs to herself. He's often late. She leans against a pillar, observing people's clothes, watching their gestures, catching snippets of their conversations. Arrivals hall: friends fly towards one another, exclaim, embrace, move off up to the bar. Ten minutes pass. The bell rings. She scrabbles in her bag. Where the hell has William got to? She fishes out her mobile and checks her messages. Oh oh. Domestic crisis. May not make it. Sorry. Leave my ticket at the box office just in case.

Damn and blast him.

Complaining's against the rules. Their friendship depends on her tact, discretion, acceptance of his other commitments. She's agreed to these rules. They've begun to feel like a net of ropes: far too strong, confining her. They've begun to feel like a rope bridge over the abyss: far too fragile.

She first met William at a talk he gave in Wilton's Music Hall near Aldgate. She peeps into the main theatre, draped in white sheets and set with painters' trestles, she steps over yellow coils of cables. She joins the queue that filters into a low-ceilinged square space alongside the auditorium, shadowy, a makeshift bar in one corner. Walls stripped back to plaster, ready for restoration, make a backdrop for a host of keen profiles. The bareness and plainness of the containing place, the absence of defining modern décor, releases them all into the past. Timeless: we could be in the nineteenth-century; the eighteenth. Everybody looks alert, smiling. Everybody seems to feel that exhilaration of imagined flight; that freedom to mind-move, shed old ideas, try on new ones. Talking to his rapt audience, charming them with jokes, William is focused, keen. Dark blue eyes, big nose, springy hair, long fingers. Eighteenth-century street life; he describes and analyses it, conjures it using the letter D: dirt, disorder, disgust, dissolution, depravity, dread, dress, dreams, debts.

She goes to hear him talk a second time, in a West End bookshop. Afterwards, while he signs copies of his book, chats to the crowd of fans clutching purchases, she lolls against the counter near the till. Posing. He comes up with his glass of white wine, halts in front of her. He is gathered, energetic, and all this energy crackles between his hands; he holds the electric air, a bouquet he offers her. He tells her about his writing. After three glasses of wine she begins to feel like a writer herself. They talk of Dr Johnson's night walks through London with Boswell, with Savage. They discuss the flâneur in French cities; the male stroller of boulevards. They quote Baudelaire at each other. They twist words into new arrangements, little bits of speech, hand them back and forth. Little pleated notes. Paper darts she launches at him. They swivel through air; he catches them.

The emails begin a day later, and hook her. She falls not into love so much as into deprivation. Recently divorced; her lid slammed shut; and suddenly someone bangs at her darkness; the ceiling lifts off and she sits up bewildered, lightheaded. Hunger awakes which he cannot recognise or satisfy. Email her dose, her drug. He measures himself out sparingly drop by drop, amusing, affectionate, careful not to compromise himself. Inside herself Polly outlines him in gold. She illuminates him, haloes him. She buys all his books, reads them carefully.

She answers his emails too quickly. She's too eager for contact, thinks about him too much. Avalanches of words she tries to hold back but can't. Her responses flow: jokes; anecdotes; flattery. Her fantasy of intimacy; connectedness. Outside conventional chitchat they fly free like angels. Avatars. He bumps into her in cyberspace a couple of times a week and then runs away again. She is the city and he is the underground train rumbling far beneath; invisible; shaking her walls, her streets. He rolls along a secure track: he tells her, after a while, that he lives with his wife and two daughters in a north London suburb. Her desire takes no notice; her desire's a winged golden beast, a cherubim unleashed, soaring into the sky. Not adultery she's seeking so much as conversation; as Charlotte Brontë sought it with Monsieur Heger.

The three-minute bell sounds. People surge to the back of the foyer, flow up the thickly-carpeted stairs. She finds her seat in the front row of the Circle, props her elbows on the velvet-covered parapet, peers down. The audience swirls in, restless, parading. Milling and gossiping. Those loud-voiced people in their satin flounces and ruffled shirts must be actors; pretending to be unselfconscious, expecting to be looked at, needing to be admired. Welcoming each other with exaggerated bonhomie, elaborate gestures. They subside into their seats as the lights go down, and Handel's overture begins.

The minimal set turns and wheels like a dancer: a big freestanding golden staircase up and down which characters run, from which they spill out arias. Costumes: hyper-modern. Mini skirts and stilettos for the women, jeans and leather jackets for the men. How odd if Handel's first audience back in the eighteenth-century saw these get-ups: whatever would they have made of them? Futuristic nonsense, perhaps they'd have called them. Whatever the eighteenth-century word for futuristic was. The modern costumes and set make the opera timeless. Sex and greed and death given a fresh look, a fresh twist.

The music seizes her. She concentrates, hears each note precisely, at the same time dissolves, becomes part of the collective ear. She hears the parts and she hears the whole. All around her in the hushed theatre she senses other people do exactly the same, merging with one another in the blackness surrounding the tiny lit box of the stage. The audience becomes one body: the music and each other and the singing and the darkness.

Polly comes back into herself as the crimson, gold-fringed curtain sweeps down to waves of applause. Her scattered parts fly back into her and cohere. Released from her enraptured attention to the opera she yawns. Returning to the real world of the enclosed theatre she smells unwashed bodies, sour sweat, tallow candle-grease, musky scent. She wants to stretch, but her dress suddenly feels too tight for comfortable movement. As though she's put on weight during the performance. Yet her dress fitted fine when she came out; just skimming her hips.

A door behind her opens, slams shut. The flames trembling above the clumped sconces gutter and stream in the draught. She tries to twist round. Crack of a seam. The stiff bodice constrains her, like imprisoning hands placed on her ribcage, one on either side of her waist, squeezing her. Hard to breathe. Stays stiff as armour, strapped round her inside the casing of thick material, hold her upright. Strips of whalebone dig into her sides. She rises awkwardly, bends sideways to pick up her fallen gloves, pulls them on. She glances down at her dark yellow petticoat, pleated blue overskirt knobbed with clumpy bows of silver ribbons. She bunches up this bulk of satin with both hands, turns. Where's the door of the box? How does she get out? Where's her scarf? A short silky cloak hangs from her shoulders; she touches its black frilled edges doubtfully. What's going on? Surely she came out dressed in red?

All around her, in the curve of little plush boxes, ladies and gents yawn and grimace, get up from spindly gilt chairs, put on their cloaks, seize their hats, turn and make for the exit doors, whose curtains are being plucked back by footmen in red coats and breeches. Polly is alone in her box. Well, yes. Someone has stood her up, hasn't he? She does remember that much.

She follows the example of others, goes past the bewigged young man holding the door open, out into the red-lined corridor thronged with people exclaiming, laughing, chattering. Walking feels almost impossible, her feet pinching in her narrow shoes. The heels so high that she tittups, feels herself sway and tilt forwards, each step a tentative movement, toes wobbling down, calves braced and clenched, quite different from her usual stride. She goes gingerly downstairs in the press of people, one hand on the balustrade for balance in case she falls, turns her ankle.

She reaches the portico. People stare at her, a woman on her own. All the other women are hooked up to men. Like iron hooks and eyes. Polly's loose, like a dangling button. But look at that boy over there darting off, so slight in his long blue frock-coat, hat clapped to his head, big boots leaping him along, curls flying out from under his hat, long ringlets like a woman's. Freedom to run not mince, fly arrow-straight not sway, curvet. Freedom to choose the route of your getaway. Polly feels like a tent on stilts. Pegged down. She sticks out her chin, narrows her eyes to slits, proceeds on her way.

The cold air outside in the courtyard smites her face, threatens to crack the paint sealing it. She puts up a gloved hand and tests the varnished carapace of cheeks and brow, touches her lips. The glove comes away rouged at the tips. Bizarre. I don't wear red lipstick.

She shivers in her thin cloak. Too dark to see properly. Keep moving through this confusion of men in long thick overcoats, upraised hands waving torches, hoarse voices shouting, flickering lights. Horses neigh, throw up their heads, jangle their harnesses. She pushes her way out of the crowd jostling towards the rows of waiting carriages, avoids a steaming heap of straw-woven horseshit, and begins to walk along the cobbled street, high heels balancing carefully from one slippery stone to the next.

She dares, now, to think. Has she gone crazy? She seems to have travelled backwards. Fantasy. Presumably she's asleep. Just a dream. Nothing to fret about. Just keep going, stroll to the end of the dream, a long arcade, tumble out of it into your own bed. But where is home? She can't remember. She sways along, skirts gathered in one hand to keep them from trailing in the stinking mud caking the cobbles underfoot. Such an odd gait these cramping shoes force upon her. Her other hand presses against her nose, to stop the reek of rotten cabbages, fish slime, urine. The chilly wind slows and disarranges her. Her petticoats flap up like sails, her little silk cape flies about her, the feathers stuck into her hair curl down to flick painfully against her face. Her tugged curls, precariously fixed with hairpins, blow this way and that as though they'll pull free altogether, like a wig, and whirl off into the gutter. The gilt strings of her reticule tangle themselves around her wrist.

Her velvet shoes suck up the wet. These soles thin as cardboard, sodden, will disintegrate if she has to walk much further. She does remember, now, the direction she must take. She stumbles eastwards, towards the Strand. Darkness envelops her but nonetheless she feels conspicuous in these strange clothes. She walks as quickly as she can, dodging the drunks who totter in twos and threes, lurching towards her with hands out. They catch at her clothes as she passes, curse her as she wrenches free. Fucking cunt! Bitch! She hauls herself away from their sour beer breath. Tears wet her face. What's she crying for? She ploughs on.

On the Strand she can slow down a bit, take deep breaths. She knows the way now. She's not far away from home, she's sure, without yet knowing where home is. How do you recognise home? Home leers and beckons her: come here, dearie, come with me and I'll show you a good time. She gasps, swivels, blunders on. Silver gleams of water at the end of alleys to her right. The river sends her its strong tar smell. Come on lovey, lie down with me here and I'll carry you home.

A bulk of blackness just ahead dissolves into humanity. Two men emerge from the shadows, make towards her. Talking animatedly, they don't see her. Both well-dressed, the skirts of their coats flapping, three-cornered hats clapped on their heads, bunched white cravats bright in the darkness. The shorter one, almost as wide as he is tall, bulbous nose and pockmarked red skin, his calves swelling like burly hams, wears a huge curled wig. He stumps along leaning on a black cane, wheezes as he talks. His companion, tall, big-nosed, bends towards him, eager. One slender hand gestures in the air, the other holds a sheaf of manuscript. William. There he is, after all! She lets out a cry, smiles and holds her arms wide, stumbles towards him.

When she wakes, the early light streaming through the thin curtain, her room looks exactly as she left it the evening before, books and clothes strewn about. Studio flat: the landlord's term. Polly calls it a bedsit. From her sofa-bed in the corner she checks the bookshelves, the table, the two small wicker armchairs. Red eyes of messages blink on the phone display. She jumps up, plays the messages. William rang too late, well after she started for the theatre. Blast him.

She wriggles her bare toes into the brown pile of the carpet. Not what she'd have chosen. Contemporary, the landlord called it, not wanting to bother with replacing it. Fake beech is more fashionable; pale and cold and noisy. Odd to be renting in a modern building. She and Harry lived in a flat in a ramshackle Victorian terrace in Finsbury Park before they split up. Old floorboards she painted creamy white. Cracks between the boards you lost things down. Earrings. Rings. Her wedding ring. She took it off during an argument and threw it at Harry and it rolled into a crack and disappeared. Hard to lose anything here: so little space for loss. Except inside herself.

This small room holds minimal possessions. She chose that. Stripped down. Like being a student again with two brown pottery coffee-cups, one silvery aluminium saucepan, one white pillow. Once she discovered Harry's affair she jumped up and ran off, taking just one suitcase. Harry brought over some more of her things the following week. Are you going to come back? Polly said: no, I don't think so.

Friends said on the phone: oh, you've bolted, have you? Polly the bolter. She thought she'd been cunning, outwitted pain, leaving it behind, too big to fit into her bag. She left pain no forwarding address. But pain, that smart detective, caught up with her pretty fast. Picked her heart's lock, barged in, squatted, took possession. She's learning to co-habit with pain.

She pulls on her dressing-gown, makes coffee. The

screw-top machine hisses and spits. She pours the black liquid into her big porcelain coffee cup, bought from a junk shop. Cheap because of its chipped handle and missing saucer. Around the rim coil sprays of pink and turquoise flowers, gold arabesques, linked by fine pink cross-hatching. Inside the cup's bowl, blue and pink flowers twine against a white background. A mid-nineteenth-century relic. Polly bought it as a consolation prize the day after Harry gave her his news. Living on her own she can possess one beautiful, single cup. Albeit slightly damaged; like a divorcée. Nothing needs to come in couples any more.

She carries her cup of coffee over to her table, pushes aside a heap of books, sets the cup down. She picks up her mobile and calls William.

He interrupts her when she's only two-thirds of the way through her story, when she's still picking her way down from St Martin's Lane towards the Strand. Her narrative loops and rambles too much for William's taste. Her narrative's a flâneur, idly taking its time. What's the point of this? Where's it going? Does William really want to know? He jumps in, becomes an editor; impatient, requiring plot development rather than description. He's the author. He takes over the dialogue.

You imagined it.

His deep voice sounds hoarse, as though he's spent the evening down the pub, drinking, talking till all hours, in a haze of cigarette smoke. One way to solve a domestic crisis: leave the house, leave your wife to calm down, don't come home until late. Sit with your men friends, watch football on the pub TV, buy each other pints. Peace. No one making demands on you to listen, getting angry or criticising you or belittling you, telling you you've let her down, blubbing red-faced, exaggerating, weeping she hates you. Late at night you slope home, let yourself in quietly, hope she's fallen asleep. Tomorrow is another day. Start a fresh page.

No, Polly says: it was real. That was why it was so strange.

What's real? William says: we make it up, reality. You dreamed it, that's all.

Pause. She hears the rasping strike of a match, his inhalation of smoke. She feels him gather himself up, make a real effort at contact. His voice becomes amused, caressing: oh Polly, you and your imagination.

Polly stares down at her pale green lap, her dressing-gown hanging in loose folds over her knees. A favourite garment; a flimsy version of a frock-coat. Like the coat worn by that young man loping away from the opera house last night.

Blisters on both heels twitch. She feels their hot, stretched tenderness. Those tight high heels I staggered along in. Whereas I went out in flip-flops.

Stress, William says: tell me about it.

She reads between his lines. She's become expert at this scrutinising of invisible ink. Footnotes scrawled in lemon juice. She deciphers his sub-text, holds it up to the light. He means the opposite, of course. Don't tell me now. Maybe later. Darling, don't be a nuisance. We have such fun together. Don't spoil it.

Polly, sweetheart, he says: I must go. Lots to do. Take care of yourself. Talk to you soon.

Don't expect me to take care of you, is what he means. Talk to me when I ask you to and not before, is what he means. She's a deft translator. Her intelligence awakes as her blisters throb. Wedging her mobile against her shoulder, she bends down and strokes first one heel, then the other. The blisters sob in flesh language: recognise the truth. She instructs herself: don't be stupid. Don't pretend you don't understand.

She's been a sleepwalker and now she's jerked awake. Of course she knows what's going on: how could she not? She's defenceless against this sudden onslaught of understanding. His language falls on her like sharp chips of rock, cutting her forehead. His words pierce her stomach like knives. But I asked for it, didn't I? I let it happen. I went into it eyes open. No, eyes closed. I've been such a fool.

I must go, he says: sorry.

She possesses a single needle, kept for button emergencies, stuck into a reel of grey cotton. She pulls out the needle, sterilises it in a match flame lit from the gas, then hobbles over to the chair next to the tiny kitchen table and sits down. She twists her bare foot up onto her knee, angles her heel upwards, places finger and thumb around the blister, presses it gently inwards from both sides, to bulk it up, make it easier to stab. A little fat skin-cushion of water. She pierces it with the needle tip. A moment of resistance, and then the point eases in. A second stab. More pressure applied. Translucent liquid gushes out, flows over her heel, drips onto the floor. She flattens the loose lid of skin with her middle finger, mops the empty sac with a clean handkerchief.

Is this an eighteenth-century blister or a twenty-first-century one? How can she tell?

Stars push out of the night sky above the Strand like bright needle-pricks. The moon races in and out of indigo clouds. The two men halt, frown at her. Obviously disconcerted. Female body breaking into their minds, disrupting their rapt conversation, the brisk march of their thought. Splintering their mutual attention. She clutches her wet trailing skirts with one hand, tries to pull her skimpy cape closed with the other. Their eyes flick down at her rain-streaked finery, back up to the low neck of her dress. She's bare-headed, her hair disarranged, tumbling onto her shoulders. If she ever had a hood, it's fallen off. Her little cap too. Somewhere behind her: a bedraggled feather trodden into the dirt.

She can feel her lower lip jerking like a child's. The taller of the two men stares at her as though she's a cockroach jumped up in his path, waving her feelers at him. Or a bird of prey, hopping up to peck at his soul. His look: a spear of ice. She splits, sees herself as though she tittups across a stage: her tear-smudged painted face, the turquoise grease coating her eyelids, her absurd corseted décolleté pushing up her breasts like eggs.

She wants to explain. She knows she's in disguise. Like some sort of fancy-dress party. She opens her mouth, lifts her hand beseechingly, screeches William's name. The scream scrapes and dies in her throat. No sound comes out. Contempt tightens his face. He raises his arm, white frills falling back from his dark sleeve: the threat of a blow. He balls his hand into a fist to ward her off: don't force me to hit you. He hasn't spoken but his meaning punches her in the belly. The shorter man pushes in front of his friend, speaks almost gently. No, no, my girl, it won't do. He waves his fat hand at her. You misunderstand us: we're not customers. Polly reaches out again. Gives a pleading squeak. Now his voice saws like a rough file. Go on, be off with you, leave us alone!

His words seize her, give her a good shake, clap her between the shoulder-blades. He seizes William's arm and pushes past her. Knocked off-balance, Polly feels her knees wobble, collapse. She staggers, trips, sprawls full-length on the slimy paving-stones. The men's flapping woollen coat hems recede, the shining red heels of their shoes. Trollop in her siren finery. Pathetic, a street-walker of that age. Forty if she's a day. A short laugh, a change of tone. Now, as we were saying. Their voices fade.

Rain and tears soak her. Snot drips from her nose. No

handkerchief. Her cheek rests on a fold of sodden sack. Stinking. Not a sack: a soft horse-turd. Strange relief; lying here winded, crushed, all the pain leaked out of her. They've taken it away with them, turned her tears into words cool as marbles they can jiggle in their pockets. Just stay here till morning. Just give up. Melt into the mud. Join in, be refuse, be a dead mouse, a fouled rag, be sludge creeping down a drain. Fall asleep, drift off and never come back. Swept along the gutter, emptied into the river, drowned. Rubbish to be carried away by the tide, swirled into the sea.

She pulls herself up on bruised elbows, onto smarting knees. She stands waveringly, clutches the air to get her balance. Her high-heeled shoes have fallen off. Good. She sniffs, wipes her nose on her wet sleeve. Come on, you've done enough crying for the moment. The main thing is to get home. She hoists her skirts above her ankles, starts to plod through the mud. She tramples over it but it fights back, splashes, reaches up to her, clings damply to her legs: mud stockings. She's a mud woman in a mud petticoat. Never mind. Just get back to your mud room, your mud bed. Somehow she knows now what direction to take. Keep going east. Past Temple, past St Paul's. Find Stew Lane, that narrow alley between warehouses, find the stairs down to the river, sit on a mossy green step and wait for dawn, then find a boat-man, a boat, and go home.

She turns off the shower, lifts her aching legs out of the

bath. The mud hosed off her feet, they look tidy and white. She presses her toes onto the white bathmat. Chipped varnish. Take care of that tomorrow. For the moment, wrap herself in a towel, dab antiseptic cream onto her voided blisters, cover the white discs of skin with strips of plaster. Don clean jeans, a clean white shirt. Find a pair of shoes.

Her jewelled flip-flops, mud-encrusted, stand by the front door, side by side, at the ready. Eager to take her for a stroll; to walk her back out into the city streets; to roam with her wherever she wants to go.

Tristram and Isolde

We got back later than we expected, after the shops shut, but we didn't fret. Everything in the flat had been left ready for us: a cardboard box of dry groceries on the kitchen counter, the fridge stocked with vegetables, milk and wine, the sitting-room tidied and vacuumed, and a pile of ironed blue sheets in the cupboard. No radio mumbling, no TV flickering with the sound turned down. The place felt full of echoes. Empty. We would both have to grow larger to fill it.

Inhabiting the space with him alone made me inventive. I wanted to try out new gestures, new routes between cooker and cupboard and shelf. I crossed the kitchen floor with a dancer's steps, twirling to the ping of the microwave. We curled on the sofa together, his arm around me, and ate cashew nuts from the bowl in my lap. He poured some wine and I shared it with him, though I don't much like wine. What mattered was taking a sip from his glass. We toasted one another. Izzy, my darling, he sighed.

We slept in each other's arms all night long, my head tucked between his shoulder and chin, my legs wrapped around his. I woke from time to time, in between dreams, to feel his breath, warm and regular, brush my cheek; to feel his heartbeat. His smooth skin smelled of fresh soap, and cashew nuts, and mushrooms. We'd eaten mushrooms, black and buttery, for supper. Now their juices scented his sweat. As morning bladed the curtains he began to stir, holding me even closer. Still half asleep, I laid my face against the soft fur curling across his breast and stroked it. I encircled his waist. I held onto him and caressed him. Eyes shut, I whispered: don't go back there. I don't want you to go. I want you to stay with me. I nuzzled him, licked him, bit him gently. I said: I'm going to tie you to me with a silk ribbon, then you won't be able to leave me. Not ever. He pinched my chin and said: so you'll have to come with me then, won't you? He kissed me all over my face and I kissed him back. Together we kicked off the quilt and rolled out of bed.

I brushed my hair in front of the bathroom mirror. He liked to plunge his hands into my mop of curls, twiddle them between his fingers, rummage them about. He liked to pretend to lift me up by the tops of my ears. He said I had pointed ears, like an elf. This morning, though, we didn't play those games. He sat in the bath, knees up, whistling, while I scrubbed his golden-brown back with the string mitt well soaped with the green soap I'd given him for his birthday. We both disliked perfumed soap.

This one, egg-shaped, was made with olive oil but just smelled very clean. I liked smells, but not the sickly-sweet variety. I liked the smell of newly cut grass, bracken in hot sun, salt-crusted pebbles on the beach, creosote, fish frying, newly painted walls. Most of all I loved the way his skin smelled of what he'd just eaten. If he'd been out without me to a restaurant I could always tell, when he came home and cuddled me, what he'd had for dinner. I shut my eyes, held him tight, and sniffed him. Sometimes he smelled of lemons, sometimes of blue cheese. He didn't eat a lot of meat but if he did it came off him in a strong red whiff and I felt a wolf was hugging me.

While he talked on the phone I made breakfast. Saturday morning alone together: a feast. I decided to lay the table with the best plates, the pale pink ones that gleamed like satin. I spread the blue and white checked tablecloth, cut bread for toast and made a pot of tea, put out the butter and the marmalade. We ate porridge sprinkled with brown sugar, and two slices each of brown toast. Then he washed up while I swept the floor, shook the cloth and put the rubbish out. We locked the front door and set off. I'd tied him to me with a length of string I found in the kitchen drawer, the one where we kept matches and bits of greaseproof paper and odd nails and screws. I knotted one end around his right wrist. You see, I said: I wasn't joking. Now you can't run away and leave me. He pulled on his leash and jumped up and down and growled. He pawed me and pretended to lick my nose. Then we walked along hand in hand. Love, like sap, a green juice, coursed from his heart down his arm through our joined hands up my arm into my heart and I felt so happy I smiled at everyone we met. A bunch of violet pansies had pushed up from under a low front garden wall and was blooming in a pavement crack. I loved those pansies' courage, daring to be in the wrong place, and I loved the fact nobody had picked them or trampled on them, and I loved his warm palm enclosing mine holding love there like a gold bead.

Through the alley, onto the concrete bridge over the railway line, past the disused factories, across the graveyard and the wasteland, towards the river. Two hundred yards along the water's edge and we reached our secret place. In through the tall iron gates we went. We curved around a high hedge. The city vanished. No streets or cars. No traffic noise. Just birdsong. Broad paths of scuffed sand, soft under our feet, crisscrossed the tussocky grass. Low hills thick with bracken stretched away in every direction to the horizon's rim. We swam in pale gold rays and white mist and cold air. Well wrapped up in our jackets and scarves, we lifted our faces to the sun and felt coldness sliding under its heat. Layers of warmth and cold, delicate as a millefeuille. This morning I felt I could eat the whole world, roll it on my tongue crisp as pastry, tart and sweet as oranges.

Dogs trotted past, pursued by their owners. We nosed along like the dogs, in pursuit of our private quarry:

more time alone together. The only way to get it was to be ruthless: to run away. To avoid all the mutterers, the finger-waggers, the no-sayers. To blot them out. I didn't much care what they thought but he did. It mattered to him that we observed the forms, the decencies. He didn't want to hurt anyone. He wasn't yet ready to tell everybody how much we loved each other. He told me, though, and that was all I cared about.

I untied the string from his wrist. It had got us this far; now I no longer needed it. He was as enchanted as I by the golden day, the fresh smell of earth, the crackle of dry leaves drifting on the cool breeze, the green spaces; they tugged us forwards. We turned off the main path and entered the wood. A series of copses dotting the waving mass of bracken. Horse-chestnuts and beeches and oaks bent towards each other over our heads. We pushed through the waist-high greenery, following the deer tracks, narrow lines opening in the curled fronds that pressed up against our waists as we plunged along. Under our feet we crushed the springy ferns, releasing their sun-warmed, bittersweet scent.

He walked ahead of me because he knew the maze of tracks better than I did. I followed his dark yellow corduroy back. Deeper and deeper into the wood we went. Sometimes a jay started up, or a magpie flapped past, or a lime-green parrot turned over in a tree like a leaf. Doves and pigeons cooed out of sight. Branches moved far off in the sea of green, rippling it.

No: not branches but ears pricking up. Green and gold and brown swaying pools and currents of light coalesced into deer suddenly visible, raising their delicate necks. Nearby reared other branches, fierce and forked: horned antlers. Part of the forest transformed itself into a red stag. He turned to look at us. On his head he bore his antlers like a tall crown, a candelabra of bone. All wreathed with streamers of green fern. He was a stag and he was the king of the wood. My knees wanted to fold. I wanted to fall down and put my forehead on the ground and salute him. I stood very still. He reared his head and hollered. A great cry wrenched out of him, answered far away: another stag, invisible, bellowing back.

His herd of female deer stepped out, slender and stately, sunspotted; rocking forwards silkily like boats. He marshalled them, kept them together. They didn't mind our presence; they were used to us, to our hands empty of weapons. People who knew no better, men with enormous cameras, crept far too close to the deer, bothering them, and the stag raised his head and roared, warning them off. The men with cameras thought they could possess the deer by taking pictures of them. You couldn't. They didn't let themselves be captured. They preferred to flee. The deer swirled with the stag away into the forest. They melted back into sun-dappled greenery, they became part of it again and vanished.

We reached our destination: a particular oak tree in the heart of the plantation. Very tall, with ribbed black bark framing the entry to its hollow trunk. We had discovered it a year ago; the dark interior invited us to climb in. Our secret room. Inside, we stood packed together, a close fit; a double vein of green sap. Two green stems plaited together. My face against his jacket, our hands in each other's pockets. You're the green man, I whispered: and I'm the green woman. Like the chapter in Tristram and Isolde where they run away together into the forest and live there secretly. To myself I whispered: we're married now, I've tied you to me, I've knotted us together for ever and ever. I knew, of course, that like Tristram he was married to someone else, Iseult of the white hands, queen of the kitchen in her white rubber gloves, but that didn't matter. I was his real wife, the one he secretly loved best. She wasn't here now, was she? She was far away and she couldn't see what we were doing.

He took the length of string out of my pocket and twined it into a circle and crowned me with it. His arms hugged me round. He said: we're very attached to each other aren't we! Laughing. I breathed him in: ferns and sweat and soap and tea.

We clambered out of the hollow trunk, squinting in the sunlight, brushing bits of bark off ourselves. We climbed up the tree. He made his joined hands into a ladder step for me and tossed me up onto the lowest branch. I caught it and swung myself up and he came after me. Up and up we went, piercing into greenness, rustling sun-burnished leaves beneath us and above us and all around us. Well hidden now: no one would ever find us here. The deer passing below might scent us, the ants zigzagging along branches run over us, the pigeons perch on us, but no human being would ever guess our presence. We'd climbed out of the human world and vanished into the heavens. Our sky-kingdom; just him and myself and the beating heart of the tree. He sat astride one branch, his back against the main trunk of the oak, and I straddled another a little higher up, swinging my booted feet back and forth over his knees. For a long time we sat like that, listening to the sounds of the wood, not speaking. From time to time he reached up with his hand and grasped my boot and gave it a little punch and pushed it gently to and fro.

The warmth of the sun deepened under my jacket, my skin. My thoughts floated like leaves rafting down. We could live here as long as we chose. We could gather dry branches and twigs for fires. For food we could roast acorns and chestnuts, nibble grass and the soft tips of ferns, shoot foxes and pigeons and squirrels. Either we'd sleep in the forked branches of the tree or else we'd make a bed of bracken under it. We could weave the bracken into green camouflage coats to hide us when we went hunting. We could stick feathers into our hair to disguise ourselves as birds. Nobody would ever find us, however long they searched, because we'd hide so high up in the tree. We'd hold our breath when the searchers came past: they'd never guess what strange creatures nested between tree-top and blue sky. He and I together made one single creature of shared love, shared thoughts, hands clasped, eyes fastened together, we completed each other, we were enough, we were all we needed, we belonged together and would never part.

I told him all this inside my mind. I didn't need to talk it out in words. I poured my love into him and he poured his into me, we were a single flow of sweetness that went back and forth. Time stopped, didn't matter; our green world held us. The tree's green arms. Just we two, our circle, in drowsy golden light and warmth.

He shouted. The world broke in two and the fragments flying apart hit me in the face in the mouth in the teeth. I put my hands over my face to protect myself from arrowing shattered glass. He shouted: fuck just look at the time! I couldn't speak, couldn't look at him. He cried: come on, Izzy darling, time to go, I'll give you a hand down. The sky blunted my open mouth. I hated him so much I swayed and rocked, nearly fainted.

Lovers have to part. Lovers have to snatch the time when they can meet. Lovers don't have long enough together. Lovers complain and grumble and cry.

Especially secret lovers. Outlaw lovers. We could float in our green treetop world outside time and feel free there but sooner or later a mobile would bleep and summon us back to streets and hospital wards and that wrinkled grub in the white plastic cot next to her bed. I grizzled, stomping along behind him. He grabbed my hand and towed me back into the street, towards the bus stop. He put on a fake charming voice so that all the old ladies on the bus would think aaah what a good father he is. You want to see Mummy, don't you, Izzy darling? And your new little brother? Of course you do. Last night they were both so tired but this morning they'll give you a big smile. And you'll give them one back, won't you?

Sooner or later people came and caught you and you were found out and punished. It was your fault. What you'd imagined was too terrible ever to be mentioned so you just buried it in the hollow trunk of the oak tree under a heap of leaves where it could rot and be forgotten about and you were the oak tree hollow inside nothing inside you but a secret going bad going more rotten by the day emptiness powdery dry and grey as ash.

Mummy said: did you find the frozen pizzas, love?

I kicked the leg of the baby's cot, jiggling it, and the baby woke up and started to howl. The cry wrapped itself around my ribs like ribbons drawn tight threatening to stop my breathing.

Sunshine fell onto the white cream paint of the windowsill, as it did in the kitchen at home where, a black bulk against the light, she spent so much time bending at the sink, her back to me, the radio on the shelf chitter-chattering.

Now Mummy leaned over, picked up the baby, fastened it to her breast. She said to Daddy: did you remember to bring the video camera, darling?

The metal window, pushed open, let in cool air to the hospital room. I breathed out so hard that the ribbons binding me broke and I leaped high up in the air and became invisible, I leaped up to the windowsill, balanced, concentrated then jumped, flew out, across the city streets down towards the river the bridge back into the green park. I landed softly. I trotted fast along the tracks, swerving into the green-gold bracken to avoid dogs and walkers, I made towards the woods. In dappled light, whiteness playing with darkness, dancing and overlapping, I could merge with the waving bronze undergrowth, become apparent, dissolve again, and so I became my new, true self, hoisting my antler coronet wreathed with ferns, bearing it with lightness and grace, calling to my deer to surround me then vanishing with them into the heart of the forest.

Honeymoon Blues

Vomit gains its shape from the throat, arches out in obedience to the curve of that narrow tunnel, that ripple of muscle. Porridgy spout, flecked with red bits. Like the sandwich spread of childhood, scooped on knife-point from small jars: creamy glue of salad cream, red and orange specks of vegetable all mixed up: pre-digested. Mealy fountain, a warm uprising; you gasp, gag, let go. Sick: a deliverance; your insides rush outside and fall at your feet. The point of getting drunk: to discover, then practise, that sensation: going beyond your limits; losing control. Out of it.

Maud leans against the pebble-dashed wall of the pub, fingers idly splayed to stroke and test its surface of grit lumpy as congealed sick. She watches the revellers. The warmth of the day has summoned the teenage girls, turned them into half-naked nymphs prancing bare-limbed in halter-neck tops and tiny shorts; the city street a beach. By nightfall, hair dishevelled, arms and faces burnt pink, they stagger; but still determined; towards the next bright bottle. Summer heightens the desire for ecstasy, for throwing up. Maenads celebrate their rites, lurch along arm in arm, weaving wild garlands of insults and endearments they hurl at passersby. They jeer at Maud then rock past. Vomit splatters the pavement just in front of her. A rosette of sick on each of her toes? No thanks. Hey, she shouts, and slams away from the unsteady chorus-line, into the smoky pub.

She drinks pale yellow wine. Smeared glass. Corner table haloed by cigarette smoke. High stools rim the horseshoe-shaped bar. Tealights sparkle on the windowsills. The big ceiling fan rotates.

She drains her glass, smacks it down. She pushes back her wooden chair, stands up. Is she drunk? Death grins and says yes. Death nips forward smartly, grabs her arm, tugs her into the street. The ground tilts, tipping her off the world. She's out in the wasteland stumbling over a mountain of landfill, a high wind blowing rubbish at her face, the wind scours her bare shoulders, she's lost. On the horizon, large wild dogs stand still, watching her intently. They wait. They edge nearer. She backs away. Aha, she mutters: fooled you. I'm off to catch a plane.

They land in Venice at dusk. She hurries out of the chilled airport, walled by glassed-in ads; lean and hungry women, fake breasts pumped up, smouldering in metallic underwear; into humidity, onto the bus, with its sticky plastic seats, mosquitoes whining in just before the doors slam shut. At Piazzale Roma she takes the water bus along the Canal Grande. She can't let herself look out at the water, the palaces. She stays gladly shut in by the throng of people. The bus rocks up to her stop. She gets off.

She pads through the darkness, tugging her wheeled bag along. It glides behind her like a memory. Why not just abandon it? Buy different clothes here, assume a new identity, a disguise. Big dark glasses, red wig, leopardskin wrap, stiletto heels. Become transformed. No more a woman who suffers. No more loss no more hunger no more need. Coming abroad you leave your old self behind; you shed skins. Strip off those wornout states of mind. Stride out claim what she wants go for it buy it. The ghosts of all the new women she could become shout at her from the magazines she flicked through on the plane, their wispy portraits printed just behind her eyes.

She halts in a small campo. Alleys mouth in all directions. She concentrates, then picks the right one, recognising the bakery on the corner, the little box-like shrine to the Madonna next to it. Plaster mother wears a crown of pink plastic peonies, braces her bouncing boy on her blue-draped hip. When the metal blinds clatter up in the morning, revealing the freshly stocked glass shelves, she'll offer him sugared cakes, buns, sfogliatelle; leaves of golden pastry delicate as air.

Round the corner. There's the pilastered doorway. She recognises the scrawl of the yellow neon sign above.

Up the three steps into the cramped hotel Reception, she lugs herself and her case. Smarter and cleaner than formerly: gilt-framed flower paintings on the marble walls, gilt octopus chandelier, potted palms. The yawning young man at the desk flicks his eyes up and down her, drags out a smile, pushes the register forward. I thought you weren't coming. I was just about to lock up. She jiggles her keys in her hand: room 59.

Suitcase in one hand, she walks up to the fifth floor without a pause, just to prove she can. The staircase of white marble braces the lift shaft, turning at right angles around it. The edges of the steps shine, crisp as pleated paper. Sheets of paper on which to write love letters; white pages smooth as the sheets on a bed. The stairs rise up over her head: white-crested waves.

Fifth floor. Gloom. Smell of disinfectant and bleach. She presses a button sunk in a rubber surround. Nippled breast. A feeble light flickers on. Narrow corridor running between grey walls. Marble floor, speckled black, pink and grey.

Where the hell is room 59? The damn room does not exist. Up and down the long corridor Maud walks, searching. A slow ricochet. She passes and re-passes the lift and the stairs. From this half-way point the corridor stretches away in both directions, running towards room 51 at one end and at the other end room 58, a floor-length mirror just beyond it, set at right angles. She patrols up and down, eyeing the blank wall next to room

51, the tall mirror at the far end. The corridor plays with her, sends her back and forth like a shuttlecock, mocks her, like a boisterous father tossing a fractious child from hand to hand put me down put me down.

That child struggled then ran. She frowns. No longer quite sure of the child's name. Edges melt and dissolve. She holds a thousand words inside her, all dancing up and down. Disorderly sentences. All the words ever spoken. All the words of her past long as a corridor big as a hotel. Inside her outside her. Bits of lost time flow back to her, envelop her. Wrap her up. The hotel feels abandoned, hushed. Held in a trance of silence. As though swathed in gauze.

How long has she dawdled here, walking up and down? What time is it? She has completely forgotten. The middle of the night? Dawn? Where is she? Can't remember. Doesn't matter. She could be anywhere. Skating over marble, an aeroplane taxi-ing along a runway ready to rise abruptly up into the clouds, never come back.

Maud's limbs loosen. Weightless. Treading water. Should she feel scared? Such strangeness. Burden of worry has slipped from her shoulders; gone. She feels relaxed, dreamy. She yawns. Plenty of time.

The light breaks up all around her, dances in tiny scintillating points like diamond dust, like the tiny bubbles on a foam bath taken in a dark room lit only by a candle. Glittering. Like being under the sea, somehow, in a jewelled cavern of coral flashing and sparkling in underwater light. Language swims around her, fish darting back and forth wriggling their tails. Words shimmer. A strange landscape. She's walking through her dreams. Is that it? Not quite sure. She's awake, but walking in the layer of waking called reverie. Some sort of altered state. The light shifts and twinkles; deep-sea stars.

Walking in the unconscious, is that it? A fugue state. Odd. Not frightening. Just peculiar. She dissolves. Just made of pinpricks of light. Words. Lost. Wandering through the city of her unconscious.

Not a city at all. Indoors. Inside this hotel. This corridor.

Eventually, hazily, she works out where to go.

That big mirror at the end of the corridor: not a mirror but the frame of an aperture, an opening, offering not a reflection but holding air in its grip. Marking a corner. The corridor obviously continues around it.

She steps forwards, plunges through the dark doorway like dark glass.

The light behind her goes out. Night surrounds her, presses onto her face. Don't move. Under her feet a pool of blackness. Supposing the floor stops just here, an open trapdoor, she'll fall down the hole, fall through nothingness, into the room below, onto its marble floor, splatter of brains and blood. Suppose the corridor ends in blackness, an open door onto open space, she'll walk straight out of it, fall out into the night sky, tilt towards nothingness, whistle down onto the street four storeys below. Rockabye baby on the treetop when the wind blows the cradle will rock when the bough breaks the cradle will fall down will come baby cradle and all.

Dark air solidifies into a wall an inch from her nose. Sharp, right-angled turn. The corridor seizes her, picks her up, carries her along. A short passageway, with room 59 at the end of it.

Maud shoves the key into the lock, twists it, falls through the door, sends her suitcase slithering across what must be lino, flicks down the light switch.

Surprisingly un-modern décor. Pure 1970s. Green, purple and silver whorls of wallpaper. Double bed with leopardskin-covered headboard and orange chenille counterpane, veneer wardrobe, scarlet formica table on splayed aluminium legs, fragile chair with chocolate velvet puff seat patterned with sunflowers.

The bed nearly fills the room. She edges around it, to the window veiled in white nylon curtains. Parting these, pushing apart the metal shutters, peering through the gap, she makes out, in the darkness, some sort of balcony or *loggia*. On its far side, arches frame blocks of indigo sky freckled with stars.

Two red dots, like glow-worms, bloom just ahead. The tips of cigarettes?

She closes the shutters and draws the curtains. Unpack. Just the items she needs to get her through the night. Half bottle of whisky. Box of sleeping pills. She fingers the dimpled layers, each packed in silvery plastic. Little poppers, little press-studs of oblivion. She pushes one out. Little bullet she shoots into her brain. Then a slug of whisky. She won't think about that strange experience just now in the hotel corridor. Just accept it; forget it.

She undresses, climbs into bed. The sweet mask-face of a Madonna floats above her, calm and still. High forehead veiled in transparent cream muslin. Hooded eyes gaze down at the Gesu paddling in her blue lap. Her long forefinger tilts towards his pursed red lips reaching for the pearlike breast peeking from a slit in her dress. The gap of longing: mother for baby boy and baby boy for mother. Between them, joining them: comfort and certainty; they can bear to hold separation between them, like a rattle, like a silver spoon. Maud climbs up the sharp rocks towards her mother, falls back, starts her climb again. Manna in the desert. Tower of ivory. Mouth like a rose. Fount of sweetness. Fountain of milk and honey. Star of the sea. Tom. Gone.

Groggily peeped at in the morning light, the little *loggia* looks scruffy and neglected. A sort of outdoor cupboard. Withered stumps of geraniums in pots, a stack of plastic crates, some empty wine demi-johns, a bench, a saucer of cigarette ends on a three-legged stool. Perhaps the receptionist sits there for a quick fag in between shifts. Perhaps that's where Maud should sit, later on today, supposing she's brave enough to empty the box of pills down her throat, sluiced along with the rest of the bottle of whisky. First of all, though, get dressed. The least you can do. Self-respect to the very last.

On their first morning here she and Tom went out for breakfast. Between the shadowed buildings light falls down like white arrows. Brilliant slices of street. Emerging from a dark *calle* chosen at random they blink back into sunlight, a large *campo*. On the far side: an uprush of white stone church; wall of sheer white. In front: a tall hexagonal fountain; slabs of white marble faced with reliefs, a circle dance of goddesses, satyrs and nymphs. Iron railings topped with spikes surround and dwarf it. The water's been switched off. The fountain's lifeless; dry.

Maud and Tom walk hand in hand. She teeters in stilettos, a tight sleeveless dress, white with black polka dots, pinioning her knees. They sit down at a silver aluminium table outside a café, behind a low hedge of dusty box bushes in terracotta pots. The seat of her chair, metal and chilly, strikes through the thin cotton moulding her thighs. Her body so warm from bed, their recent embraces. Canopy of blue sky overhead. Smell of vanilla and hot sugar, of dust. Behind them, inside the café, the fierce hiss and spurt of the espresso machine. Tom bites at a fat croissant-like bun. Yellow jam shoots out. He stirs sugar into his cappuccino and licks brown froth off his spoon. Maud jiggles her chair out of the shade so that golden light caresses her face and arms, smoothes the back of her neck. The world is a warm hand stroking her.

Over their two honeymoon weeks she learns about Tom's appetite, which matches her own. A church or a palace or a roomful of paintings, a stroll over the strobe of canals and little hump-backed bridges, and then he begins feeling hungry again. I'm starving. Quick, let's have lunch. Big, sturdy man exaggerating to make her laugh.

Onto the Zattere, onto the big wooden raft floating between brilliant blue sky and its reflection in brilliant blue water. They choose a table at the far edge of the raft, close to the serving trolley with its racks of cruets, piled tablecloths, bread baskets. Pink napkin spread over her lap, bottle of white wine chilling in the ice bucket, platter of seafood and fish between them. Crisp golden rings of deep-fried squid. Salt and oil and lemon on her tongue. Sips of icy white wine. Mounds of crab cupped by a reddish-purple radicchio leaf. Coral, scarlet and cream flesh on a dark blue china plate on a pink tablecloth. Sun gleams down onto the coarse linen weave, the curved steel of forks. Maud moves her arm out of the shadow cast by the sunshade, rests it on the tablecloth in the sunshine. Sun like a hot brand strikes her flesh, clings to it.

*

Maud, alone in her hotel room, lifts up her hands and looks at them. Ringless brown fingers. She remembers Tom's brown skin. Like a cloak he wrapped her in. Bye baby bunting daddy's gone a hunting gone to get a rabbit skin to wrap the baby bunting in. They went into each other; vanished inside each other. Otter, she called him, and seal, and horse-chestnut. They couldn't stop touching each other. As soon as she got near Tom she wanted to put her hands inside his clothes. They'd get dressed in the mornings then tear their clothes off all over again. Such appetite for each other, and for glasses of wine and grapes and peaches in bed, and for shared baths, and then for more sex.

Pain, that gourmand, feels hungry, jumps onto Maud, plunges into her, nibbles her insides with pointed teeth. Pain gnaws her with gusto, an army of mice chewing on wainscot. She stares at her bag, slumped on the floor in front of the wardrobe, wonders what to wear. What to be discovered in. She banishes the pain in her belly by ignoring it. Remembers the rules of deportment taught by the nuns at school; sucks in her stomach and stands up straight. Shoulders back, head up, bottom tucked under, stomach pulled in. No slouching! She has not become one of those round-shouldered slumped women, bellies loosely poking forwards, faces soft as margarine, whom the magazines deplore and berate, who trundle around clothes shops like lost parcels. She's not lost. She is not she is not. She's just a little empty that's all.

*

After-lunch siestas are euphemisms for sex. Sweat-perfumed sex, bump of the headboard against the wall, creak creak of the springs, crying out into the pillow so as not to disturb the guests next door. Her sleeveless red top and red cheesecloth skirt lie crumpled on the lino where she has dropped them, tangled up with Tom's white t-shirt and blue jeans, their clothes making love, shadow selves wrestling on the floor.

They've married soon after first meeting at a conference in North Wales on radical publishing. Maud spots Tom, likes the look of him, bumps into him deliberately as they queue for their institutional dinner, and they take it from there. Over glutinous prunes Tom tells her: all women are goddesses. A drink in the bar turns into a few, then a couple more. Tom puts her, late at night, into his car, and sets off to the hills, inland from the sea. You don't know Wales? Wait till you see this. He parks in the middle of a forest, jumps out, holds the door open for her. Come on, come and see. Above: the full moon, somehow voluptuous, white light pooling down onto the tops of bushes. Tom darts between trees and Maud follows. She takes off her sandals in order to go barefoot. Her soles touch coolness. They sink, then spring up again. Densely curled fibres tickle her arches. She bounds over sopping moss. From mound to mound. To push into a strange forest in the night: she's never done this. But Tom's with her and knows the way. She has a guide. Moonlight whitens the path. Tom takes her sandals from her, tucks them into his jacket pocket. Late summer evening. Juicy earth, soaked, bearing her up; tussocks she leaps between; rainwater squirting between her toes.

They reach the shrine to the saint. A stone well, square. A cistern. A tiny house. Maud lies on the shelf of rock jutting out above the deep water. A stone windowsill. She's a fish in a cupboard. She has arched out, dived into the night, and now readies herself, poised, to re-enter her element. Tipsy, all right. Cheap red wine still burning inside her. She's peeled off all restraint along with her sandals.

Not a saint so much as a goddess, Tom explains. Saint she may be called now, the converted Celts re-naming places as sacred to a male God, but her other, forgotten name is pre-Christian, pagan; archetype of the wild virgin loping free in the woods. Obligingly she wears her holy disguise, bears a new holy name, but otherwise remains the same: fierce; benevolent; dangerous. The powerful sweetness of this place distils more than legend: a live presence summoned by humans who need to clasp other human beings in their arms, who search for meaning, belonging, adventure. Above them: the black night and the stars, the dazzling moon.

They walk back towards the car through the white-dappled darkness. Trackless forest. A young man at her side, quoting poetry. Metaphors gushing out like jets of water from the mouths of dolphins on fountains. The moonlight falls on her like a blessing. It strokes her bare arms like silk. The forest smells of wet earth and bracken, of mushrooms.

Tom's dead. Maud's arms close on air. Her open mouth kisses nothing. She wants to scream into that nothingness and then lie down on the railway lines in front of an approaching train and beg it to mash her to red pulp, but she behaves. You have to. You have to keep going. For the sake of the children, the family, your friends, everybody else. So you keep going to work, and you drink rather too much, and you decide to go back to Venice, and you carefully pack your overdose, just in case, and you worry you're going mad. Too much on your own. Too lonely. This hotel's too quiet. Probably she should go out for breakfast, into the fresh air. Sit in a bar in the *campo* and order coffee. Look at passersby. Feel part of the crowd.

But she can hear voices. Soft laughter. Maud pads, naked, across to the window, peers idly out. She jumps, grabs a fold of nylon curtain and swathes it round herself. Just outside, in the little *loggia* walled by white sunlight, a young man and woman, their backs to her, sit entwined on a small bench. Her fair head on his shoulder. Their feet up on the balustrade of the *loggia.* On the right, a French window stands open. The young couple must have come through there from the room beyond.

The young man shifts his position. The girl taps out a cigarette from a packet, offers it to him.

Maud backs away, pulls the metal concertina shutters

to, disentangles herself from the rope of nylon curtain. She picks up her blue lace blouse. She loathes its short, ribbon-edged sleeves, its pearl buttons. So tasteful. So discreet. Self-hatred woven into a blouse. Why did she buy it? Because it was cheap, because she was depressed, because she thought a widow ought to wear a tasteful blouse. She drops it onto the floor.

A baby begins howling somewhere out of sight. No, the baby claws and bellows inside Maud. Maud's the baby. Some ancient hunger revived. Starvation. Screaming has no effect on the shut fountain of milk. Cold and indifferent; closing the door. World of milk gone, arrows of black spiked railings, of barbed wire, attack her insides, tear her apart. Love will never come again love will never return she's desperate and raging flying apart exploding into shreds of flesh falling down the black pit alone for ever forgotten about rattling in empty space she'll die here and no one will ever know, no one will ever come and feed her. She'll die. The Madonna has fled, flattened into a painting. The starving baby shrivels, shrinks to the size of a pea.

She plumps down onto the edge of the bed, hands around her knees, head bowed, trembling. Wanting to be sick. Like those teenagers outside the pub, spewing arcs of milky curds into the gutter. Their friends hold their heads. Hold on tight sweetie hold on. Let me swallow the pills. Anything to stop this pain. The pills my lovers count them out one by one into my palm kiss pain goodbye.

She balances the little podded sheet of pills in the palm of her hand. She drops them. They scatter across the floor. So much for that fantasy. That melodrama. Coward. I'm not even brave enough to kill myself. Pain boils over. Tears surge out, rip her face apart. Torrent of water, hot drops scorching down her cheeks. She gropes for a handkerchief, blows her nose, blinks her swollen eyelids, mops her eyes.

Under the door slides the smell of hot soapy water. Clatter of a tin bucket. The growling song of a charwoman hard at work.

Don't give up just yet. For God's sake woman, where's your self-respect? Who's that talking? One of the nuns at convent school. One of the lay-sisters, on all fours next to her aluminium bucket of lukewarm water and soda, face down over her scrubbing brush, circling its bristles over red tiles for the teaching nuns to mince across. Or the charwoman here on the fifth floor of the hotel, who pushes herself through her grinding work by singing, who paces herself, step by step, in a brave contralto, banging along the corridor with her mop, whacking at dirt.

Maud takes a deep breath, sighs, shuts her eyes. Let go of Tom. That 1970s honeymoon in this room. Drop memory. Put it away for a bit. Pack it up, dear suitcase. Slide it, dear memory, under the bed.

Accordingly she yawns, opens her eyes to the present, surveys the stark modern décor of her white-walled hotel room, its sleek contemporary furniture, pale blue silk counterpane. She strolls to the window, pushes aside the muslin blind, re-opens the shutters, looks out at the *loggia* again. Sunlight whitens its stone walls.

Night after night she sat there entwined with Tom, smoking a last cigarette, sipping duty-free whisky out of tooth mugs, watching the bats flick past. They liked the *loggia*'s shabbiness; part of its charm. Feet up on the balustrade. His hand in hers. Planning their future, their babies, their work. Then they'd crush out their cigarette stubs in the bucket of sand and go inside to bed.

Since those days the *loggia* has been restored; tidied up and swept; all the rubbish cleared away; the French windows re-painted. Now silvery tin planters of little box trees line the far side, and terracotta pots of pink and red geraniums march along the balustrade. The open arches framing the blue sky stand up, re-pointed, creamy stone wreathed in the green tendrils of clematis thick with mauve blossoms, climbing rose branches studded with pink blooms.

The baby howls. The baby's name: Maud. She's got to pick herself up. Nobody else will do it. You're a grown-up. Mother yourself. Try to, anyway. Approach that baby, that scratchy imp, so desperate, body contorted like wrought iron, hands curled into nailed claws, child twisted so far past desperation that she will spit at you rather than take the spoon between her lips. Lift the baby into your arms, rock her, feed her. Well, at least look at her. Recognise her.

So easy to believe she's got no power, she's just the spiky child, disliked and abandoned, for whom help will never come. So easy to stay stuck in suffering. Wrap it round her like a grey quilt. Let it suffocate her. Oh, you big baby, Maud mutters.

Courage, mon ami: le diable est mort. One of Tom's sayings, that. OK, Maud. Blow your nose again, for a start.

She walks back to the window and stares out. A good spot. Belonging to the past. Memories of love. It did happen. It was true. Memory dashes in, flying blue-black flash, sharp-winged swallow piercing in from the open sky, zipping about the *loggia*, trampolining on a branch of climbing rose, darting and swooping back and forth between the shelter of the *loggia* roof and the open space of the blue sky beyond, tying them together with loops of flight, tying Maud into the morning.

Time to walk back through the frame of the mirror; along the corridor. Time to re-enter the city outside, pain held like a baby on her hip; jiggled; soothed. For the moment; until hunger pricks, and loneliness, and the child stretches its mouth wide and starts bawling again.

Remembering George Sand

When we came blinking out of the gloomy church into the sunshine and saw my cousin Pietro waiting outside I felt blessed and important. I knew he wanted to indulge himself, talk to me about George Sand. I was the only person with whom he could do that.

My mother greeted him then began chatting to her acquaintances, a bunch of old ladies, all widows. I hated listening to their gossip about deathbeds. I hated looking at their puffy yellowish caps, like poisonous mushrooms, draped in black lace, dingy under big hoods; their sparrow bodies bundled up in thick woollen capes, their black-mittened hands clutching prayer-books. I hated widows. Now that my mother had become a widow she had become sucked into their company, they drained all the colour out of her, they feasted on her like ghouls because she was still young and pretty and they couldn't bear it. They wanted her to become like them, cracked and shrivelled with stained teeth.

I could tell, from their pecking glances, their avid eyes, that my mother was boasting discreetly about Pietro, his fine prospects, the well-off foreigners he'd been treating recently. Madame Sand, you know, the famous novelist from Paris! She didn't explain to them that Mme Sand called herself by a man's name: George. They'd have been shocked. I could not stand their nodding and hissing, so moved to Pietro's side. We dropped behind and walked together. Our whole group turned onto the Zattere and strolled there, up and down. The beginning of February and suddenly you felt the spring stealing in, changing everything, waking us up from our winter sleep. As though Venice were an enormous room, newly cleaned, windows flung open, smelling of soap and starch and freshly-washed bed-curtains flapping in the cold wind. With the fogs lifted off and the mists cleared away the city sprang out renewed. Across the blue water the dome of the Redentore sparkled in the sunlight. The stacked roofs of the Giudecca gleamed.

We walked between island and island, between sky and water, between ground and sky. The world pressed at my mouth: a promise of greenness and flowers. The golden air leaped with the clang of church bells and the scent of hot chocolate and yeast drifted out of the café we were passing and I glimpsed a basket of pomegranates standing on its counter. I wanted to bite one, hold the sweet red seeds between my teeth.

Pietro had on a new coat of dark blue wool. His boots shone burnished as chestnuts. His hair and beard, curled and oiled, seemed somehow exuberant. He bent towards me and said: dear Giulia, I am glad to see you so blooming. After these past weeks of nursing Mme Sand so devotedly your mind must live under a strain.

Not at all, I said: on the contrary, I am very well.

I stood with him inside a blue egg, just before it cracked. The blue sky stretched up and around us, a blue membrane, blue as the dome of the church we'd just left, that inner skin painted with visions of the Virgin. A holy day, Sunday, because I walked with my dear cousin along the side of the Zattere, the sun stroking me and the breeze a layer of coolness on top of it, and the blue of the water reflecting the blue of the sky.

Of course I helped him: my kinsman, Dottore Pagello. My mother certainly approved of my helping a lady in misfortune, because you never knew what might come of it. Contacts. Introductions. A leg up in the world somehow. Pietro, when he first solicited my help in caring for the foreign invalid, did not tell my mother that the lady in misfortune travelled accompanied by a young man not her husband. He assured mother that Mme Sand was a good person, wellborn and rich, and that was all mother needed to know.

Pietro took my arm and smiled. His thick hair sprang up around his head. He looked like one of the knights on the fresco in the church we'd visited together on New

Year's Day when we went out for a walk in the late morning. That dark little church smelled of dust and rot and mould, but Pietro smelled of lemony hair oil and was completely alive. Just behind him the painted knight hefted his lance in one mailed fist, the other clutching his horse's bridle. I felt glad that Pietro was not trapped stilly in colours on a wall but could steer me out back into the sunshine. Later on that day, I saw Pietro for the second time, when he arrived to have supper with mother and myself. After supper I went for another stroll with him, to see him half way back to his lodgings, before turning back myself and making for home again. We paused outside the Danieli, admiring the torches flaring outside the huge entrance doors, their flames streaming up into the night sky. Pietro said: one day I'll be as rich as any of those people taking rooms there, just you wait and see, little Giulia.

I didn't know, then, who'd just arrived at the Danieli. While Pietro talked of his ambition, Mme Sand was perhaps standing in her bedroom pulling the long pins out of her black hair, shaking it down over her shoulders, putting on a loose wrapper and comfortable slippers, curling up on her sofa, cutting a few pages of a new book, losing herself in reading, then calling for servants to fetch her a glass of wine, bring her hot water for a bath.

My memories of her are bright as playing cards snapped from the pack and slapped down on black cloth.

But memories hurt too much when they shoulder in unannounced. I need to stay in control of them, flick through the pack, shuffle and deal at my own rhythm. How to put all the memories in order, though? Begin at the beginning, that's all. Simple as that.

So. I first saw George Sand in early January soon after she arrived in Venice with her companion Alfred de Musset and took rooms in the Danieli Hotel. She described to me later her rapture at arriving in the evening, waking out of a headache-filled sleep to find herself in a gondola gliding up to Piazza San Marco, the dark water ribboned with gold reflections of light, San Marco itself black as a cut-out against the immense moon. So utterly romantic, she sighed, smiling at her own need for a dramatic beginning to her tale. Falling in love with Alfred in Paris. Escaping with him to the city of dreams. How commonplace foreigners' imaginings are! Venice is my city. That is all I need to say.

I acted as Pietro's messenger when she asked the hotel to summon her a doctor. I often helped Pietro by running his errands; I enjoyed knowing he found me useful. In response to her plea he sent me round to the Danieli with a note, and a little basket of blue winter pansies. The liveried footmen in the entrance hall nodded me through to the back stairs. I ran up, knocked at the door pointed out by a chambermaid, received no reply, gingerly stepped into a tiny hallway hung with heavy drapery. I pushed aside the fringed pink brocade curtain with one hand. Across the warm, musk-scented room, dull rose satin, lined with lace, fell in festoons from the tall windows, obscuring the grey sky. I peered into the dim space at what seemed a white cloud. A gleam of white muslin.

I made out her shape. Wearing a white wrapper, its voluminous sleeves rolled up above her elbows, she was sitting at the little desk in the corner, writing and smoking. Her back to the room, as though saying: I don't really inhabit this place. Her black hair, piled up on her head, a coral spike thrust through the toppling knot to secure it, formed her untidy student's cap. One thick curl, escaped, hung down on her white neck. She seemed far away, across an acre of flowered pink and blue carpet.

She smelled of attar of roses and of tobacco. Blue smoke wreathed up in quick little spurts and spirals from her armchair. One bare foot stretched out to rest on an embroidered stool. Two high-heeled green satin mules flopped on their sides nearby, as though she'd kicked them off and left them where they fell.

A small round table, draped in a white lace cloth, stood near the chair, holding the debris of her breakfast: broken apart brioches, a pink porcelain coffee pot painted with flowers and scrolled with gold, a matching pink coffee cup, wide and deep, a small blue glass vase of black twigs dangling greenish-yellow catkins. The flick of an eye let me trace the scent of roses to the bedroom. The door stood ajar, revealing the shining curve of a zinc bathtub. Tossed over its edge: a white and red striped towel, its lace end dangling. She told me herself, some days later, that she used attar of roses bath oil. She'd brought it with her from Paris.

How odd this remembering is. My mind darts at the recent past, those moments of existence lost and gone, tries to get at it, wrench it back, but the past flees like wraiths of mist above the lagoon. Remembering re-embodies the past, that's to say makes it up at the same time. I've always thought, up until now, that memory dwelled quietly inside us, like piles of sheets and tablecloths in the linen-cupboard. You might not see the cloths but you'd know they were there: you've helped hem and mark them, count them back from the wash, iron and fold them, as I've done with mother hundreds of times. So then, when you needed a cloth, you'd simply open the cupboard door and choose the cloth you wanted. Now I realise that's impossible. I open the door and the cloths and sheets fly up with a life of their own, burst into the room, tangle about in a mad dance, threaten to overwhelm me, twist around my throat and choke me. My memories don't belong to me. They are as unruly as children. (As the child I was. That child I dimly remember. So wild she was.) Yet the name George Sand points to more than just an event in my life. That name, branded on me, scorches my flesh, hardens to a round red scar. That name burns in my memory, like a hole charred in a cloth. The blackened smouldering edges of the hole tell me she was there. I fill in the blank. I darn and patch the sheet. I wash it, starch it, iron it, fold it up, put it away. A damaged sheet that I have mended. That I have rescued and re-made.

I hovered in the doorway, under the dusty pink canopy, and looked at her, as I was to do so many times. When I looked at her I often forgot myself. I seemed, when I came to afterwards, to have dissolved into her, fascinated by her. I emptied myself into her, became part of her story. I couldn't keep myself apart from her so I didn't really think about what she looked like. Now, if I try to remember her, to describe her, I end up making a list: I see her in parts, in bits that do not join up and can't convey her charm. All my list does is enumerate: that full-lipped mouth of hers, that long-fingered hand holding a pen, that pen seeming an indissoluble part of her body, an extension of it, like an extra organ; that arched foot tensely outstretched. Those huge dark eyes, which I saw for the first time when I obeyed her summons – *vieni qua* (in very oddly accented Italian) – and walked forwards, around the chair, and faced her. Those black ringlets hanging down, thick and glossy, on either side of her pale face. That round chin. That white wrapper sashed with a man's scarf.

She threw down her pen and immediately began complaining. Her contralto voice spoke the Italian words in an odd singsong. I couldn't eat the pastries, she said:

the vanilla cream is too rich. I'm feeling very unwell. I've got a migraine. Is the doctor coming? I asked the housekeeper to send me a doctor.

I curtsied, held out the basket of pansies so that she could see the note sticking out of one corner, and said: Dottore Pagello sent me to tell the gentle Signora that he'll be with her as soon as possible.

Behind me the door smacked open. I turned round. A young man erupted in. That day, of course, I didn't know his name. Later I called him Alfred the poet-thunderbolt. He shook himself out of his wet greatcoat, dropped it on the floor. Water gleamed on the dark cloth, ran off onto the parquet. I had an impression of height, broad shoulders, fair hair, a red mouth in a golden beard. Like a red fruit in a golden tree.

Where have you been? George burst out in French: you've been gone all night!

He ran his hands through his dishevelled hair. His cheeks were flushed, his eyes bloodshot and unfocused. I couldn't sleep for worrying about you, darling, he said: I've been walking around the streets, trying to calm myself. Don't start reproaching me, I can't bear it!

He flung off into the bedroom. Tears rose and shone in her black eyes, spilled over, ran down her face. I thought I'd better leave them to it.

Pietro duly came in later on to bleed her. The migraine departed but she went down with dysentery. She hid in her bed for two weeks. Pietro could do little for her, now, when he visited. He sat beside her bed and tried to rally her with bracing phrases, words he shook out onto his palm like freshly-rolled pills. He tried this dose and that, while I watched and listened; his little assistant with hands folded in her lap. He told her he'd seen her at her window here on the night of her arrival, a beautiful, exotic-looking stranger staring out at the glittering night from a gold frame, a gold oblong of blazing candlelight. He'd immediately entered the hotel to enquire who she was. She smiled weakly but she was too ill for compliments. The wrong medicine. Too sweet: she gagged on them. I leave you in very capable hands, he said, indicating me. He winked at me and I shook my head at him and whispered in dialect: you liar, you storyteller!

She just had to ride the illness out; endure it. You didn't need a doctor for that. You needed a nurse who didn't flinch at what she was required to do. Since Pietro requested it, I came in to help nurse her when needed. She refused to have nuns caring for her; she didn't like nuns. I daresay they would not have liked her. She didn't like the hired nurse we found, either. She preferred me. So, a sort of apprentice nun, I took over the nurse's duties. I assisted her on and off the commode, lifting her, lifting her nightgown and bunching it around her waist, lowering her onto the seat. She held on to my shoulders, panting. Then she'd jerk, she'd gasp, her face went pale green, she shut her eyes, sweat sprang out on her brow, she'd clutch my arm and convulse, as each pulse of shit left her and she shuddered. Sometimes she laid her arms around my neck, rested her face against me, sobbing. I'm so sorry, she kept gasping: I'm so ashamed. I soothed her: it's all right, it's all right.

So she should have been sorry, I wasn't born to do that work, I wasn't brought up to work as a nursemaid wiping filthy arses, I've got better things to do with my spare time! What worried me was getting her shit on my apron or on my hands: that brought us too close, somehow. And her shit, because of the dysentery, seemed so very alive, leaping out of her in torrents. I worried about dropping her too, as I manoeuvred her to stand up again and lean against me; I wiped her soiled flanks with a dampened towel with one hand and steadied her with the other; we lurched in an unsteady *pas de deux*. Then I'd imagine Pietro praising my nursing skills, his eyes bright with gratitude, and I'd calm down, I'd murmur to her as my mother murmured to me when I had the stomach ache, I'd pat her dry, I'd help her back to bed. She'd collapse into it as though I'd shot her. Each day I washed her, put her into fresh nightgowns, changed her sheets. I carried away the foul, swilling pots from the commode and left them at the top of the backstairs for the slaveys to find.

My job ended there, thank heavens. I'd go home, and write a short note for Pietro, describing her state, I can't say progress. He needed to know how his patient went on, even as he scurried about attending other ill people. As soon as she felt a little better, he promised, he would come and visit her again, and prescribe medicines to see her through her convalescence. I took her these messages. They didn't mean much to her: she could not believe she would ever get well.

During this fortnight, when her body lost its edges and dissolved into puddles of brown liquid, Alfred vanished into the streets of the city. At first, not knowing any better, I simply assumed he had a poet's quivering rawness to life's hurts. My mind glossed him softly: the outer skin of his soul seemed very fine, easily punctured by the barbs of others' pain. He could not bear to see his beloved mistress suffering. He feared she'd die. He needed her to stay strong, to recover. To witness her helplessness, to see her weak as an infant, incapable of attending to anything but her own distress, desolated him. He went out to escape from the sick-room atmosphere, the stuffiness of the shuttered rooms, the smell of the eucalyptus we burned in a tiny brazier to keep worse smells at bay. Who could blame him? I certainly did not. Instead I pitied and admired his exquisite sensibility.

Sometimes, in between sightseeing excursions, he dawdled around in the salon, and I'd sit with him for ten minutes, pleased to have some company, while he described the Venice he was discovering as a tourist. He haunted picture-galleries, churches, museums. He made sketches. He went to concerts. He found a way of introducing himself to Venetians, I supposed; he made friends. Desperate with anxiety and grief, he tried to distract himself. Poor young man, I thought. Poor poet. He'd come to Venice on a kind of honeymoon but the woman he adored had vanished and in her place had appeared this ashen-faced invalid. She disgusted herself. She made me douse her in lavender water in case she smelled bad. She sent me off to wash myself very carefully after attending her onto the commode. Her voice drifted after me I'm so sorry so sorry.

As she mended, so she began to talk to me. She tossed out pieces of her history to me like sweets. I fell for her romance of herself. I didn't realise, for some time, that in telling me about herself she was simply testing out versions of stories on a rapt audience. She veiled the truth, I see now, much as she liked to appear transparent and pour out her feelings. She gave me chapter after chapter of her life story, on those January afternoons, during her convalescence, when I came to keep her company, and I hadn't wit enough to see that her story chapters did not add up, they formed a glittering array of glass bits, a mosaic she constantly broke up and re-formed.

She told me once she had dreamed, en route to Venice, that she was turning into a mosaic; carefully she counted her little squares of lapis lazuli and jasper. That dream was indeed a self-portrait. The selves she presented were all artful, artificial; like elaborate costumes. Mere masks of paint like courtesans' faces made up for Carnival. As a good courtesan would, she adapted her stories to suit her audience. How much I must have amused her, hanging on her words open-mouthed and stupid. Perhaps she enjoyed keeping me tied to her, tied to her stories. Perhaps she enjoyed teasing me. Torturing me.

One way to understand her better, during her illness, was to study her belongings, her clothes, even her shoes. Her possessions led to her, just as her dressing-room led to her bedroom. Occasionally, while she slept, exhausted, I perched in front of the looking-glass in her dressing-room and tried arranging my hair like hers. I rummaged among her bottles of scent, her pots of face cream, her sticks of perfumed grease. I sniffed at them. I dabbed my neck and wrists with attar of roses. Such a plenty of comforts! Such wealth to lavish upon cosseting her person. Such expensive luggage. She travelled with a dressing-case of inlaid mahogany fastened with a brass clasp, sockets lined with red velvet sewn with ribbons to loop through her tortoiseshell combs, her rings. I'd never seen anything so luxurious. I stroked the velvet, fingered the rings.

I'd heard her tell Pietro she preferred to live a simple life. For example, she'd come to Italy without a maid. So what? She couldn't pull on her own stockings now. And since elegant simplicity meant travelling with only two night gowns I'd had to go out and buy her more. (How ever did she afford the Danieli's prices? Very simple and very exorbitant.) I lifted then re-folded her chemises. I wondered where she'd had her underclothes made. Paris, I supposed. I fingered the tiny hem-stitches rolling the edges of her lawn handkerchiefs, the lace that fringed them, the raised silk of her monogram in the corner. I stole one of these handkerchiefs. I so wanted her to give me something. Something of her own. I didn't feel bad stealing the handkerchief. She could order more. I simply took from her what I needed. The handkerchief felt like mine already, and so I took it back. I made it mine again. It joined us. It meant her-and-me. How intensely I enjoyed stealing from her! A tiny triumph. A tiny bit of power over her. My secret.

Alfred now slept in a small adjoining chamber, originally designated as his dressing-room, so as not to disturb her. Early on in her illness he had begun staying out half the night. Sometimes he didn't return until breakfast time, just as I took in the tray the maid had brought up. Pietro ordered her to drink broth, to build up her strength. The best meat broth. The best meat jelly. The hotel didn't mind having to send out for what the doctor ordered: it all went on the bill.

Mme Sand's dysentery continuing into a second week, a new terror lodged itself in Alfred's mind. When he came in from one of his night-time rambles he'd clasp my arm confidingly, as though I were his little sister, and fire urgent questions at me in a low voice for a couple of minutes. No, no, I'd reassure him day after day, she has not got cholera, she has not got typhus, she simply has dysentery, many travellers get it, she will recover very soon I promise you. Thanks, Giulia, he'd murmur, pressing my hand. Then vanish into his room to sleep.

I went on sympathising with him. Then I stopped sympathising and instead felt churned up inside, like mud at the bottom of a canal when children poke at it with long sticks to see what they can turn up. For children bits of refuse form treasures. Children's minds work magic, transforming mud-coated rubbish into gems. But my mind whispers filth filth filth. Throw this memory back down into the scummy stinking canal where it belongs.

One morning in late January, when she was beginning to mend, and could get up into her armchair in the bedroom, to doze, he came in, flushed and red-eyed as usual, but, rather than greeting me and asking after her, retired immediately to bed complaining of feverishness. Some hours later, as I sat in the salon, reading while she slept, the door to her bedroom ajar, his faint voice summoned me, asking for a glass of water.

I went in. He lay, fully dressed, on his bed, the neck of his shirt wrenched open, the sheets dishevelled all around him like waves cresting a wrecked ship. His bed was a divan, by daytime made tidy with a blue coverlet, blue cushions. Now it was scattered with loose-leaf drawings. I set the glass on the nearby table. He caught my hand, pulled me to sit down on the edge of the bed. His voice was agitated and hoarse. Talk to me just for a little while. I'm so lonely.

I began to collect up the sheets of drawings littering the coverlet. Are these your sketches? I asked. In the same moment, glancing down, I saw the drawing I held was of a naked girl, lying on her front, legs apart, buttocks raised, posed on a bed rather like this one. Alfred laughed. No, I bought those. He didn't want me to talk to him, I discovered. The other way round: he needed to talk to me. His words spewed out like vomit. That's the wrong word to use, perhaps, for vomit is disgusting and his words were only half so, they intrigued me against my will, this was a dark stream issuing from his very soul, very soon I realised I shouldn't listen but I did, I felt caught in the swirl of his sentences, he began pouring out confessions of things he should never have mentioned to me, and all the time one of his hot hands held onto mine and the other impatiently turned over the drawings. She doesn't know how to love. She's never given herself to me properly. She won't allow me that pleasure of seeing her abandon herself. She's incapable of letting go. Do you wonder I have to seek love elsewhere? I can't live without affection, without love. He released my hand for a moment and swept the drawings onto the floor, a slither of legs and breasts.

I mumbled: don't agitate yourself, I think you are ill anyway. I leaned over him, held the glass of water to his lips. Still holding onto me with one hand he waved the glass away and I put it down. I leaned back over him and wiped his sweating face with my handkerchief. He reached up, caught my ear, tugged me closer. He began stroking my face with his free hand. He caressed my cheek, my neck, my shoulder, rapidly and confidently. I let him. I'd never admit that, if I told this sin in confession. I felt my face grow warm under his touch. I tried to make my mouth protest but it wouldn't. Just a squeak came out. His skin so burning and hot: when he laid his face against mine I felt consumed by his heat. He let go of me abruptly so that he could sit up, then seized me in his arms and pulled me down onto the bed. I toppled and fell and lay next to him trapped in his arms. His breath very warm, smelling of rum; a deep sugary amber smell, dark as his flow of words, I was intoxicated, I couldn't stop listening to the words he poured out at me a sort of poetry rough and rude and angry words like whips to beat a woman with turn her backside weeping and red and raw.

I let my mouth speak as it wanted to, it wanted to find out to experience to know to understand. So where do you go to seek love? I whispered. He began coughing. Love! His voice came out low and rasping. To tarts, obviously, he said: to the same places all men visit when necessary, your sainted cousin included, in between mistresses where else should he go for fucking, a tart'll give a man real hot sex unlike that dummy next door. I tried to push him off but he was lying half on top of me, pinioning my arms. I'll tell you what I do with tarts, little Giulia darling, he whispered: you'd like that wouldn't you, I fuck them up the arse, I fuck their brains out and they adore it. He went on and on in that secret violent language until my ears felt flayed by it, I was not Pietro's pure little cousin any more just a girl with her skirts rucked up about her waist and Alfred's hand rummaging under her petticoat.

I wriggled away, out from under him. He fell back against the pillows, laughing. I stooped, picked up the glass of water, and carried it from the room. Though my knees shook I did not spill one single drop. Her voice called from the bedroom and I went in to see to her.

The weather continued chilly and wet, mist concealing the edges of the *campo*, the paving stones beneath my feet slimy with damp as I came home from the baker's. I wrapped my scarf over my mouth to fend off the dank breath of the canal smelling of rotten cabbage. I peered at its sides green with mould, the brown film on the water: you couldn't see more than a little distance ahead. At home I would wrap two shawls around me. Even with mittens on my hands felt stiff with cold.

Alfred fell ill himself, at the end of January, just as she got better. What a pair! Like the little man and the little woman on the weathercock-house, he vanishing inside just as she swung out. She recovered from dysentery and he fell ill with some nameless fever, which she thought might be a reaction to his night-time excesses in the bars: too much to drink, too little food, not enough sleep. She guessed, all right, what he'd been up to, but she didn't immediately spell it out to Pietro when he came to visit the new invalid.

Alfred couldn't frighten me now. He turned hollow-chested and thin, stooping under the weight of his purple woollen dressing-gown. When George came near him he jumped at her and clutched her, wrapped his arms tightly around her. Like a baby monkey clinging to its mother. How frail he looked. How robust she seemed now in contrast. He would nuzzle her shoulder, murmur endearments, squeeze and kiss her. Worry at her. She would pat his back, patiently, maternally, as though he were a child with colic. Then, very gently, she would push him away, disengage herself. Arms crossed over his concave chest, he would hug himself, obviously trying to control his shivering, his fever. He seemed fragile as a piece of paper fluttering in a draught from an open window.

She confided to me she feared it was Alfred's mind that was *dérangé* not just his body. You see, Giulia, he's very vulnerable. She sat in the armchair, correcting a pile of manuscript sheets, and I sat nearby, sorting pens for her. She wrote at such speed that she wore her nibs out, or they split under the pressure of her hand and spluttered ink all over the place. Nowadays she was always sending me to the stationers to buy new ones. Her voice looped on like wet ink sentences while her hand traced her thoughts in the air as much as on paper; her hand darted in the air like a bird swooping to and fro; her penbeak squawked and wrote together.

Sometimes her mind seemed to travel on two levels at once. With one layer of her mind, she re-wrote, thought about her story, scratched out mistakes, and with the other she talked to me. Talked at me, it felt like sometimes; talked past me. Her words blew by me like sheets billowing on the washing-line on the hotel roof. She needed me to be there; I was the washing-line and the clothes-pegs and she the windy dance of linen thinking it's free but needing the clothes-pegs nonetheless. Just so she acted the clothes-peg, the clothes-line for Alfred while he flew up on the billowy wings of poetry. She kept him tethered and reeled him in when necessary and kept him feeling safe. He needed someone to protect him, she told me, her hand keeping on with its scritch-scritch-scritch across the page: his mind sometimes sent him such troubling visitations. Once, walking with her in the forest at Fontainebleau (just a short while before they set out for Venice), he had fallen to the ground in terror on seeing a ghost. In broad daylight.

How did he know it was a ghost? I asked. He just insisted it was a ghost, Mme Sand said impatiently. I asked: the ghost of whom? His own ghost, she replied: the ghost looked back at him and had his own face. Such was the power over him of this hallucination I feared for his sanity, as I do now. Her hands holding the sheets of manuscript trembled. What a fool she was to love him so much. I made my voice as prosaic as possible. Perhaps, I suggested, he'd spotted his own reflection in a puddle?

She leaned forwards and patted my knee. Giulia, you're a good child. You're trying to console me, I know. But Alfred's a poet, and his daemon drives him to see realities hidden from ordinary mortals. I said nothing. My silence let her forget my presence and she returned to her correcting.

Knowing now, from her own experience, what a good doctor Pietro was, she summoned him to diagnose and prescribe for de Musset. I accompanied Pietro; by now I couldn't do without their company; his and hers. Watching them greet one another in the salon gave me a queer twist of feeling in my guts. Like a stomach ache, but a newborn one, with its very own name. Mme Sand received Pietro not as his patient but as a gracious lady, restored to her full glow of health. Also as an addict restored to her habit of cigarettes. She rolled one as she talked to Pietro. She wore a pale blue jacket, trimmed with grey rabbit fur, over her fullskirted dress. Her black hair rippled onto her shoulders. He gazed at her admiringly.

I perched on a stool in the background. Pietro leaned towards his hostess. He listened to her as she wrung her hands and confessed that her own illness had stopped her watching over Alfred, she'd been unable to prevent him falling back into all his old habits. Pietro soothed her: we'll see this through together. His smile included me: and our little helper. A nervous inflammatory fever? Alcoholic delirium? A venereal disease? Fits of madness?

An attack of typhoid? Some of these terms could be spoken in drawing-rooms and some could not. Venereal disease was not a term ladies in drawing-rooms were supposed to know. But I learned it in George's salon because finally she found the courage to toss it out to Pietro and he caught it and tossed it back, he juggled it with all the other words while I listened, while I watched.

As the crisis came on, she herself took over the night nursing. For eight days in a row she did not go to bed or change her clothes. In the mornings, when I came in to visit her, I found her white-faced and strained. She'd recount how Alfred ranted and raved, how he had delusions of attackers, she did not dare sleep for fear he'd try to hurl himself out of the window. At the peak of his illness he leapt out of bed, tore off his nightshirt, gambolled naked around the room, shouting obscenities. For a couple of days two male attendants, sent over by Pietro, helped her contain these bouts and outbursts. Good burly fellows who gripped Alfred, one on each side, and manhandled him back to bed.

Pietro's calm helped her. He spoke to her gently; he listened to all she said; he soothed her anxieties. He treated both of them: Alfred with purges and drugs, Mme Sand with the balm of understanding. During his visits I retired to Alfred's bedside, to give my cousin a chance to talk to Mme Sand undisturbed. He well understood what she herself told him: that her own nervous disposition meant sometimes she needed simply to talk, that if she could recount her anxieties and fears she would feel better.

While they talked, over cups of lime-blossom tea in the salon, I sat, with some sewing, on the far side of the door, left half open, in the little bedroom where the patient lay and sweated. How red his cheeks seemed against the white pillow. Spittle collected at the corners of his mouth, hung in gummy strings between his lips. Half-delirious, he would raise himself on one elbow and mutter furiously and the spittle would fly off in tiny clots and dangle on the edge of the yellow paisley quilt tucked round him.

Alfred disliked Pietro. He obviously felt a certain rivalry: my cousin was so goodlooking, healthy and strong. He had white teeth. Alfred's were yellowish-grey. His face had grown sunken. His beard sprouted in unkempt wisps. He quickly became jealous of my cousin's growing intimacy with his mistress. She's sitting on his knee! he'd insist: they're drinking from a single cup! Eventually I'd run to the door, to humour him, and peep round it. I'd reassure him: no indeed, no indeed, the doctor is sitting opposite Mme Sand and they are conversing so quietly solely in order not to disturb you.

Both invalids recovered sufficiently, Alfred from his physical ailments and Sand from her anxieties about his health, in time for Carnival. I saw it through their eyes, as Pietro escorted them to the festivities, despite Alfred's sulks, and my mother permitted me to accompany my cousin. Sand exclaimed at the continuing cold weather, but February is usually freezing here: I put on two pairs of woollen stockings inside my thick boots, wore one quilted skirt on top of another, a woollen scarf inside my hood, and carried a hot brick wrapped in flannel. We took a gondola from the hotel's fleet, and reclined in it, well wrapped in fur rugs, as we were expertly poled about through currents of music and fireworks and singing, through confetti battles, past quayside orchestras setting masked dancers in motion, past costumed parades, past troops of capering children in fancy dress. When it began to get dark, and turn chilly and damp, and the mists crept in from the water, Mme Sand would whisk Alfred off, so that the raw air could not catch at his throat and lungs and make him cough, but I would stay out with my cousin. Once or twice he treated me to hot chocolate in a café. Mostly we just eddied along with the crowd of revellers.

In Pietro's company I felt able to enjoy the rougher side of carnival, the excitement of mixing with strangers, waltzing with strangers, pelting strangers with plaster-dust and being pelted by them in return, walking tensely past the black mouths of alleys prepared to flee, both frightened and laughing, from the cloaked strangers who'd jump out and throw firecrackers at our ankles, try to catch us, manhandle us, demand money from Pietro and kisses from me. The game of evading captivity was to let ourselves to get lost in the fog, to dart into the street-maze, twisting rapidly through *calle* I did not recognise, to fly over unknown bridges and round corners and suddenly to find ourselves in a *campo* near home.

Mme Sand liked watching the antics of the street children, and turned into a child herself. She brought carnival masks back with her to the hotel and tried them on, acting out the scenes they suggested, playing Harlequin and Columbine in turn. Alfred forgot his troubles and joined with her in these mad romps, running, howling with laughter, from the bedroom into the salon and then into the bedroom again. Sometimes Pietro joined in, while I sat and watched. When things got too tumultuous I'd have to tug at my cousin's sleeve to remind him it was time for him to walk me home.

February ended with Alfred ill again, a relapse into his former condition, and Pietro once more in attendance. Sand told me early on that she had promised herself to take care of Alfred like a mother but her notion of mothering was a taboo one. Mothers don't normally take naked sons into their beds and stroke their limbs while feeding them pills and possets but that's what Sand did. Mothers don't usually hop from one lover to the next in the space of a few weeks but that's what Sand did.

Sooner or later, slow and stupid as I was, I was bound to discover the last twist in the story, the last knot I could smooth out into a neat finish. I made my version of the story last as long as possible but in the end I had to bow out. Sand was the mistress of stories. She won the game.

In early March she was forced to move from the Danieli to an apartment in the *calle delle Rasse* that Pietro found for her and Alfred. She'd run out of money, and she needed to finish her new book as fast as possible to replenish her coffers. I hadn't realised she earned her living from writing; I'd thought it just a rich woman's hobby. Now I discovered she took the main financial responsibility for herself and Alfred. Pietro told me. He knew the state of her affairs because she confided in him. He sent her his bills for medical attendance; also she had to pay for all Alfred's medicines and they did not come cheap. I think Alfred must have lived off a private income, or an allowance from his mother, but he had squandered his money on his amusements and now depended entirely on George.

Their new apartment was cramped and airless, with a small salon. I saw it just once. I don't remember the furnishings: my mind was on the scene before me, the play Sand acted with my cousin not caring that I was standing in the doorway and could see exactly what they did: the two masks held up on beribboned gilt sticks, the two papier-mâché faces smirking, approaching each other, the two crimsoned mouths kissing and withdrawing then kissing one another again. Seeing the masks I saw the truth and could not understand why I had not seen it before. I suppose because I wore my own mask of dear little cousin, sweet little helper. When the real truth is that I am just like they are: I desire and I have teeth and I can bite.

Watching the two masks kiss I felt my stomach clench and cramp and then tear itself in two like a sheet of paper. I turned and went away knowing they had not even noticed I was there.

Once Sand and de Musset had settled in the little apartment, Pietro discouraged me from spending so much time with them. I realise he wanted to keep me away; he wanted no witnesses to his growing intimacy with Sand, but obviously could not openly say so. Now, he said, he preferred I should stay at home, helping my mother like the dear sweet girl I was.

Pietro's idyll with George ended not long after Alfred returned to Paris and the arms of his mother. My cousin must have wondered whether his new mistress would leave him as she'd left all the men before him. Did he really imagine he could live with her in France, share her life in Paris? They did live together in Venice for a brief while. She enchanted him with her capacity to make curtains and chair-covers from lengths of material purchased in the market, to take up hammer and nails and upholster the chairs herself. He described to me, on those rare occasions when he came to visit mother and me and drew me apart to tell me his news, how Sand would squat, her mouth full of nails, tapping away at the furniture she was covering, and then leap to the table and dash off thirty pages or so. What a dear little woman! What a good little soul!

I knew she'd soon tire of Pietro. I understood that even if he didn't. I diagnosed his love sickness. He prescribed his own cure.

Sand had charm, certainly. A wellborn tart's charm. A way of listening raptly to whatever was said by whomever she was with. She knew how to beguile, how to flatter you by paying you close attention, laughing at your jokes, catching your allusions, tossing the ball of conversation back and forth. Her big black eyes first mirrored you then drowned you. Her white hands would clasp yours. Frenchwomen, she once explained to me, learn their art early, at their mother's knee, and so I suppose she was as French as they come. Her mother, who was a whore – let's not mince words – snared a rich man, the owner of a good property, and brought up her child to do the same. So what does the daughter do but abandon her husband, her two little children, and run off to Paris shrieking she wants to be an artist.

That was just her excuse for getting into men's beds. Rubbing up against artists in the hope that some of their talent would rub off onto her. Sex sex sex that was all she wrote about. All the so-called love affairs constituted her research, I suppose. The men were specimens, experiments, and when she'd had enough of them she pickled them in that small brain of hers then dissected them for her banal novels. In the beginning she had a certain success. Writing about courtesans' desires she tickled the jaded palates of her bourgeois readers, gave them – the females especially – the frissons they longed for but didn't dare obtain in real life. Pornography in petticoats, that's what she dished up. She understood people's appetites because her own were so ravening. Her novels were self-portraits. She pretended not to recognise that she was simply exposing her private parts to the world.

Under her ballooning crinoline she hid her filth. The very picture of decorum she seemed. Like the woman in that old woodcut in my book of stories, coming out of church holding her new husband's hand, her eyes bashfully cast down, and her forked tail sneaking out of her skirts to coil around her ankles. Oh, it's too late, too late cousin doctor dear. She's caught you now, that secret greedy mouth of hers will grab you and suck you in and swallow you and you'll drown in her foul juice. A sort of cesspit: that's what Sand is like. So many men have used her, jerked off into her, wiped themselves on her.

Since she was a hypocrite she couldn't admit what she got up to. She preferred to think of herself as a rebel, a free spirit, a romantic who gave up all for love, a passionate soul, a liberated woman. All she liberated herself to do was to take her twitchy need around the city and blare about it like a foghorn on legs. Every time she got itchy and needed a man she declared she was in love. Those poor idiots. I feel sorry for them. She called them her lovers. Sighs and tears, rapturous swoonings, tragic goodbyes, and then out of the door and digging her nails into the next pretty boy, locking her fat lips onto the next juicy bit of prey. Cooing oh darling but we'll still be friends you know I still love you in a very special way forgive me darling you know I never meant to hurt you. Each man she caught she subsequently betrayed, prancing off with the next in line. She was a bitch, simply. A bitch in perpetual heat. Women like that get put in hospital, in the asylum. I don't know why she wasn't.

I miss talking to her; listening to her and being listened to in return. I miss the way she made me feel she was so fond of me. That I mattered.

I miss you too, Pietro. I hate you as well. You encouraged me to have hopes, you used me, you used my devotion, and then you abandoned me because you no longer needed me. My affection was useful to you for a certain period. It kept you warm in between mistresses. It helped you towards your next mistress, that was all. You'd never have married me. I realise that now.

In truth what I want to utter is a lament. I'm crying. I've lost Sand and I've lost you. No end to this torment unless I end it. No end to this story unless I declare the end.

Easy as ABC

Nana, let me tell you a story.

Once upon a time a girl was born in a small town far from the capital. Her parents named her Eva. They were poor; never took holidays and never went anywhere. The local factory closed when she was sixteen. She went to stay with friends of her cousin in the city. Call us auntie and uncle, they said. They bought her some new clothes, got her onto the books of an agency, found her a job as an au pair working abroad. London. That name marked the beginning of her new life; the beginning of her new story.

Nana, do you remember? The girl likes hiding inside your coat. She twists your black button, opens your black wool front door, gets inside with you, leans fastened up against your heart, lives with you in the house of your coat. The girl could do with your coat today, in this cold weather. She shivers in her silver mini skirt and yellow halter top. Skimpy white nylon jacket can't warm her. Yellow high heels carry her away. The girl lives two centimetres in front of me. The girl is my coat. I hide in her. I live inside her. I curl up tight inside the girl inside this car.

I don't need to feel scared, leaving home. I feel brave and capable. I'm clever, I'm blonde and pretty, I can speak English. I know I'll make good money over there. How nice you look, my new auntie said, smiling. People will love you, said my new uncle. I twirled round for them.

We shudder along the motorway, lorries on either side shouldering by throwing up rain and dirt, windscreen wipers swishing back and forth. My hands want to fly out and say slow down. The car trembles. My uncle hammers along in the fast lane, keeping his place in this motorway race. The other cars come much too close. Bumper to bumper we chase each other along black tarmac slick with rain, water lashing the windows. I slump down in my seat. Walls of lorries graze past us at impossible speeds.

Inside myself I say goodbye to my parents, my childhood, my old life, packed up for safety and left behind. I said goodbye to you, Nana, long ago. I travel light, with my new pink makeup case, my change of new clothes. When we reach the airport my uncle will buy me a phone. I say goodbye to my uncle's house, his brown leather slippers on the orange rug, my auntie's porcelain dolls in frilly skirts in a row on the cabinet. Plum velvet curtains drawn at four o'clock in the afternoon, TV on, a game show, auntie goes out to the shops, uncle pours me a big glass of cherry liqueur. He says he is sure I will do very well.

Adam, Abel, Adrian, Alexei, Amos, Angelo, Apollo, Arthur, Aziz, Ben, Benoit, Bill, Brian, Bruno, Cain, Cal, Carl, Charles, Clarence, Clive, Christopher, Dan, David, Dinos, Edward, Eugene,

Nana, my uncle did not buy me a phone on the way to the airport. Stupid me to believe anything anyone said. I did not know any better. Now I do. For example, I know how much a human being costs. Not much let me tell you. Not in this grubby house. Soot from the street below coats the windowsills and the towels are small and grey.

You made me feel precious. You bought me presents. Do you remember that Russian doll? You gave her to me on my tenth birthday. Five dolls, really, one inside the other. The biggest one wears a yellow shawl with red dots, tied over her red hair, a yellow bow knotted just beneath her chin, she wears a white blouse embroidered with sprays of green leaves, and a crimson shawl, patterned with pink roses, over her coral skirt. Her wide-open green eyes see everything that is going on.

Nana, how strange, I thought I'd lost her but that doll's with me here. She sees the men enter her room, one by one. She sees the men enter her, one by one. A quick screw, they call it. Hi, doll, they say, one after the other entering the room, entering the doll. They like playing with dolls. They unscrew the doll, to find the smaller doll hiding inside. They want a doll who's young as possible.

You see, Nana, ha ha, they don't find the youngest doll of all because she hides inside her bigger sister. Screw my sister not me! They seize her, hands grip her waist, untwist her, yank her this way and that, pull her apart. Smash and grab job. Into her insides. They throw the two wooden halves onto the floor. Like two halves of a walnut shell. She's their succulent nut dipped in salt then crunched between their teeth. They want her to swallow them down she wants to spit them out.

After the men screw her the doll screws herself back together again. Nobody knows where Eva hides deep inside, many layers inside the biggest doll. They can't see her. She nails on a fake name, a fake identity, she screws on a fake mouth that squeaks yes please screw me, fake wooden lips that wait two minutes then squeak with pleasure ooh ooh ooh what a lovely screw thank you so much.

The men beat at her heart with their fists: open up, hurry up, let me in. They can go on knocking for all eternity and she'll never let on she's hiding there behind the locked and bolted door. The men break down her outer door, never her inner door. They don't know it's there. Much too stupid to find it. She's got a hiding-place, a secret place, a safe house. Behind the wooden shell that curves around her heart. While the men screw her big sister, the tiny doll vanishes. The men don't notice: too busy hammering open the wooden casing of the biggest doll. The tiny doll bends her head, concentrates, remembers your name. Nana. She taps with her forefinger on the bedstead. Creak-creak. Creak-creak. Creak-creak. A door opens inside her wooden heart, revealing a spiral staircase. Down it she runs, into your kitchen.

Nothing's changed, d'you see? Here you are, Nana, shaving curls of butter off the cold block, the knife in your hand flicks as though it's whittling, then you arrange butter spirals on a pressed-glass dish. You grasp the loaf of fennel-scented bread, saw off slices thick enough to satisfy my appetite. You open a pot of the raspberry jam I helped you make last summer. Later on we'll go to the cinema. We'll button ourselves into our thick coats, pull on our woollen gloves, and set off together. What film shall we see? Your turn to decide tonight, Nana. Something funny would be nice. Something to make us laugh.

Fernando, Frank, Fred, George, Guy, Gregoire, Hal, Hamlet, Harry, Hubert, Hugh, Humphrey, Ivan, Jack, Jake, James, Janos, Jasper, Jeremy, Jerry, Jesus, John, Karl, Kaspar, Keith, Larry, Lee,

*

Nana, I think of all the people I used to know, all those people who are gone. As though they're dead. Everyone in my family. In our town. All the children with whom I went to school. All the people I knew.

Beginning with you. If I don't think of you very often you too will vanish and then indeed I shall be lost for ever. You lie with my mother and father, my cousins, the butcher the baker the candlestick maker, my schoolfellows, white-wrapped, in the store-room one floor above this one. You're all very quiet up there but sometimes I hear you rustle in the dark. Swaddled in white bandages. White and good as shelled beans or peeled cloves of garlic. Clean and at peace.

You keep what you love inside you. You taught me that. Before you died you whispered: I shall be with you always. Telling me stories. Telling me off for telling fibs. Telling me never to take drugs. Too late to listen to you now. The drugs are my darlings and kiss me like you used to do.

I like my beloved dead to stay still and neat as we pupils were supposed to at school, children at long benches and desks. Then I can remember who's who, get it all lined up straight. No fear that some disobedient dead person will break loose, skip my rollcall, lurch out to find freedom, fresh air. In your places, children! I teach my dead their lessons for the day. E is for Eva and for Everyone, for Easy, for Empty, for Eternity. E is for the ecstasy the drug promises, E is for the end of anxiety, the end of terror.

Eva, I say to my dear dead ones, bending over them: I am Eva. Repeat after me. Tell me you haven't forgotten me. Tell me I am still alive.

If they make a noise, kick up a fuss, I will tie them tighter, that's all. Or put my hand on the back of their heads and smash their faces forward onto their pillows, muffling their mouths, their cries. Children are little savages and must be taught to behave. A child who repeatedly disobeys will find herself locked in the sitting-room for an hour with her uncle with nothing to look at but the porcelain feet of dolls. While he sticks his thing into her, his hairy hand clamped over her mouth so she can't scream, she can count dead white china toes.

The dead cannot harm you, or me either for that matter. They lie docile and still. They are all scoured-out. Dry and cracked as sweet-pea pods that have shot their seeds. Twisted into spirals and erupted: crack! Scatter of black pellets over the garden, to root where they fall. They ought to control themselves better but they can't. Not their fault. By nature they are bursting with seeds and juice and cum and it's the fault of girls if they go too far.

I was a girl once. Long ago. My uncle, the huntsman, wore a coat of animal skins. I wore a dress woven of nettles. Around my wrists I wore bracelets of thorns. Anklets of bramble spikes. I hid in the shed so that the men wouldn't find me when they rode by, their dogs yelping.

At night I undid the catch on the shed door, released and shook out my wings, and flew out of the garden into the village.

The kitchen window in my uncle's house, a small square, let in little light even at noon. Now, as the rain began, darkness obscured the glass. Night at midday.

He came home to get out of the wet, to eat. He was in a foul temper.

Lightning flashed twice outside, just beyond the little frame of the window: the eyes of a giant uncle who lay flat on the ground and peeped in and winked at me glitteringly. The house a toy in his fist. He shook me and rattled me. I was a box he wanted to open. Inside me, a pebble, bouncing between my metal sides. To him a jewel, because he couldn't get at it. Anything he hadn't got he wanted. Don't let him prise off my lid: if he did I'd go to waste. Once the air rushed in I'd spoil. I'd empty myself out. Be nothing left.

Don't let him get it. Put metal between my precious insides and the world. Put on a metal dress to enclose me so that I can't fall out.

Like a can-opener. Tin of mackerel. Grip, point forwards, jerk forwards, back and forth, seesaw, jaggedly opening it up. He split me open like a mackerel. He cut up through my belly. He slit me and my insides fell out.

Do you see, Nana, I am doing my best to put it into words, rows of words in neat, clean lines. Quiet as those dead I hold inside, upstairs in me.

When I point at one of you, stand up, recite the pronouns you know, the verbs I taught you to conjugate.

I am. I am. I still am. You are. You are Nana. We are. We still are.

The men are not are not are not. They are and they are and they are but they are not they are not they are not.

Mark, Max, Maurice, Melvin, Mick, Mohammed, Nat, Ned, Neville, Olly, Paul, Peter, Petros, Pierre, Piero, Pietro,

Nana, you want me to tell you what my life is like here in the English sex-house? Why? You think you can help me? I think you are too far away to be able to do that.

Someone else can tell you. One of the dolls. Some of the dolls can speak. You press a button in their backs and they talk. The words come out as a squeak but you can hear them if you listen properly. A sort of recording. It fades out, you press their button again, they utter it over and over until they wear out and you stamp on them, kick them into the corner, throw them away. We are disposable, Nana, don't you see? We're all much alike. We have to pretend we're not, of course. Different costumes different bodies different cunts all the same fuck fuck fuck but of course pretending to be different pretending it'll be even better this time. Some men need a new fuck each time a new body and some men want their favourites over and over again it all comes to the same thing.

Funnily enough some of the men ask me what it's like

to be me. They care about me. They know I am a human being. They want to talk not just fuck me. They want to tell me their names: all through the alphabet, Aldo to Simon to William to Zachariah. They want to know, these nice men who fuck me, how I feel.

Sure, says the doll called cuntmouth: I'll tell you. I really like touching men. I really like sex with strangers. I really like a lot of sex with a lot of different men every day. I really like being penetrated so often that I always have cystitis. I really like lying. I really like faking. I really like no one knowing who I am. I really like the way the men tell me about how lonely they are, the way they believe me when I thank them for being interested in me. I really like the way they don't notice I hate them.

I really like being an item on a shopping list. Designer shirts designer gadgets designer porn sites designer doll.

I really like remembering how my uncle took off his trousers and underpants fingered cold cream into me shoved his thing into me cold and hard as the spout of a tea-kettle long and hard with a pointed tip shove shove shove shove shove shove shove shove then he jerked and it was over so you could say it was nothing really it didn't last long but it was not nothing his bit of body did not belong in me but he shoved it into me he put it there and so I am going to get it out I don't know how yet I will have to cut him off me cut him out of me somehow.

You were saying, Nana?

*

Quentin, Rab, Razza, Robert, Roger, Roland, Samir, Sebastian, Seth, Simon, Solomon, Tadeusz, Terry, Thomas, Tim, Tom, Tubby,

You can't stop me talking to you, Nana. You hide from me but I can touch you with my words. My words are the wings of magical birds, aeroplanes, text messages, flying me to you. Rafts. Canoes. Whatever it takes. I swim through icy words, through silences. I stagger onto a foreign shore.

Today's my birthday. Apparently cuntmouth is still alive. Dazed by the drugs but still here in this ugly room. Thick scent, nylon lace bedspread. I have discovered from one of the men who fucks me that I am in the very centre of London. Apparently I'm near chip shops, kebab shops, amusement arcades, a railway station. Only the clients know I'm here. I'm a secret hidden inside a disguised house near a cheap hotel.

Since it's my birthday I should be getting a present but you've forgotten me, Nana. You used to buy me drawing books and coloured pens, and you'd dress up my birthday parcels in bright scraps of crêpe paper stuck with silver stars. You'd dress me up too, help me make costumes for the shows I did for you in your kitchen. Tutus created from pleated newspaper painted in water-colours, your nightdress as queen's robe, an upturned colander as crown. My present to you: my dancing, swaggering child self. Troublemaker. Pick me up and scold me, please.

I'd like to send you a present. I'd like to hide myself in the parcel and post myself out. If I send you myself for safe keeping then my other self can keep working here, smooth and polished and willing. The smooth self is the one they want. The sex toy. The blow-up sex doll. She doesn't cry or make a mess. I have perfected the art of falseness, which has become real. I'm all replica.

I must get myself to you somehow. I don't dare ask one of the other girls to help me. I don't know whether any of these men who say they like me wants to help me. Their birthday present to me: to fuck me. They choose me from the 'shop' here. The array of photographs. This one will do. That one won't: her tits aren't big enough. That other one's too fat. The men assume we don't care about anything. We shock the men: we're so hard, we have no feelings, we're indifferent, we don't give a toss. All we care about is money and drugs. I am going to escape from here. I'll manage it somehow. See you soon, Nana.

Ulysses, Victor, Vivian, Walt, William, Willy, Wim, Zachariah, Zak, Zebedee,

Sleepers

The train gathers speed, rocks us into the night. Adèle, flopping across my lap, has already fallen asleep, head pillowed on the illustrated paper I stole from Mrs Fairfax.

Poor motherless child. That's what they murmured, those ladies who saw us onto the train. The Hay Churchwomen's Benevolent Guild, proper upstanding Protestant gentlewomen decked out in rusty black bonnets, darned woollen gloves, solid boots. What do those dowdy do-gooders know about anything? Mademoiselle Adèle hasn't lacked for a mother. If anything she's suffered from having too many. At the last count she's had three. Four if you include me. And I'm the most faithful of them all. The only one who hasn't abandoned her.

The train rattles over the points. We bump and sway. I haven't yet pulled down the blind. Blackness outside the carriage window, beaded and trickled with silvery wet. Smell of damp cloth and leather and mothballs. Adèle's breath smells of childhood, of the milk and buns I fed her at dusk before boarding the train at Keighley.

We're gathering speed. Fleeing south, towards the Channel. Leaving Thornfield Hall, that smoking ruin, behind. Yet the memories have clambered aboard with us. They sit ranged opposite, a row of menacing mothers with thin black veils stretched over their faces. I shift into the corner. Don't look at me! I want to be the watcher. Not the watched.

Darkness falls across us like the wing of a great bird. Like a feathered cloak. The wings of a black swan flying over Paris, brought down with a single shot. Adèle's mother wore such a cloak to the opera the night after she met Edward Rochester. His first gift. Much too long for her; she had to hold it up in both hands to ensure she didn't trip. A newcomer to Paris, he tried to impress her with vulgar presents: a diamond pendant, a pair of horses, that feather cloak. Black and furry and soft. Nine months later, because it was gone out of fashion and already a little shabby, she lined the cradle with it. Later it lined the child's cot. Once laid in that downy nest in the afternoons little Adèle consented to sleep.

Such a cranky child! Fussing over her food. Greedy. Always on the lookout for sweet things. Buttery things. Pastry. Croissants and pains-au-chocolat and marzipan tarts. Four spoonfuls of sugar in her coffee as soon as my back was turned. My job was to teach her better, so that she wouldn't get fat, and hard going it was too. Occasionally I'd have to slap her and lock her in the cupboard. Children are like pet dogs; you have to train them not to make a mess, not to make a noise. In the end, though, she learned to behave. She did me credit.

Sometimes, after dinner, her mother would send for her to come and make her curtsy to the gentlemen in the salon. I'd sweep a wet sponge over her face and neck, dip my fingers in water then brisk up her limp curls. Then I'd dress her. Pink satin frock, with a very full gathered skirt, white lace mittens, black satin ballet shoes. The gentlemen liked to see her dance, to hear her sing or recite verses. She crossed her little hands and pointed her little foot and bounded from side to side. She pirouetted and curtsied. In her childish lisp she sang the bawdy songs they taught her. She sang with such innocence that they roared with laughter. Little doll, they called her: little puppet, little princess, and took her up in their arms and caressed her, *petite coquette*, *petite coquine*, and tossed her from one to the other and popped sugared almonds into her mouth while her mother looked on and smiled and pouted and frowned and finally stamped her foot and declared Adèle would be spoiled, that was quite enough, Sophie, Sophie, where are you, take her away.

Adèle copied her mother, sucked up compliments like syrup. What child wouldn't sulk when suddenly the gentlemen grew bored with stroking her, shooed her off, turned back to Madame, and I had to whisk her out of the door and bundle her up to bed? Of course she felt upset. Too much of a shock: first they heated her up with sweetmeats and cuddles until she was flushed as a peach and squeaking like a pet canary; next, without warning, their cold hands dropped her onto the floor like a used rag. I can't stand the sound of children crying. It breaks you apart inside. So I'd shake her and smack her to make her stop and sometimes I'd have to put her to bed without a nightlight and without saying prayers. She learned to be more docile eventually.

The train rocks us onwards. A cradle on rails. Perhaps I'll sleep tonight. Perhaps I won't have bad dreams.

Adèle's second mother, I suppose, was the governess. That white-faced girl, so thin and plain you'd never have thought she could get a man at all, let alone one as rich and haughty as Monsieur Rochester. Some of the servants at Thornfield whispered how wily she'd been, to catch him; others whispered she'd not been wily enough. Why else did she run away and abandon poor Adèle, if not to get rid of a baby? I thought she'd tickled Monsieur Rochester's fancy because she'd been a challenge. She couldn't charm him, as Adèle's mother had done. She'd no idea how to soothe a gentleman with a soft cheek laid against his, how to surprise him and spring into tiny unexpected spurts of childlike spirit, how to provoke him with silences, tantalise him with the curve of a bare shoulder, an eye veiled with dark lashes. She didn't know how to dress, or walk; she couldn't play the piano or sing or dance. But she could talk, all right, and stamp her foot at him. She whetted his appetite: a little woman who stood up to him, who was worth conquering, worth breaking to bridle. Too many women gave in to him too easily. Where was the sport in that?

Mademoiselle Eyre looked after Adèle very well, I must admit. She kept lessons easy and short, and allowed plenty of half-holidays. She let Adèle climb onto her lap and cuddle her, call her *ma chère amie, ma bonne petite maman.* With clasped hands I watched the carry-on. In my black frock and frilled white apron I was a dummy, that's all; invisible. Like certain other women in that cold mansion. Like Leah, the sour-faced housemaid who collected the chamberpots every morning, fetched them down the backstairs; like the various village women who came in to scrub. Like Madam Fairfax the housekeeper, poring over the toilettes in her magazines, those illustrated papers cast off by the ladies who came to visit, lonely Madam Fairfax sighing over the serialised stories, worrying about what would happen when she got too old to work. We servants were the secret life of the house, we ran about like mice behind the wainscot, we tunnelled between rooms, we knew most things that went on. Witnesses. Invisible as ghosts. Invisible as Grace Poole, the sewing-woman, who worked in the locked room on the third storey. Invisible as her charge: the lunatic girl. Invisible as my own mother, dead of typhoid at twenty-four years old. All right for the rich: they just buy themselves new mothers.

Night flees past the window. I'm shivering. Only one scanty rug between us. Adèle's fast asleep.

In Thornfield's windswept garden, in which only the toughest of flowers could survive, huddling in narrow beds, we practised deportment, mincing up and down the gravelled paths. Adèle always insisted on taking my hand, clinging onto it as though otherwise I'd run away. She exasperated me. Wrapping her arms about my waist, laying her head against me: d'you love me Sophie do you do you? I'd push her off. Down, Adèle, down. She was a spoiled puppy all right, a lapdog, a dog forever pushing its wet nose into your hand, a stupid dog that never gives up hoping you want its company. Walk nicely, I instructed her. Head up, shoulders back, imagine we're on the Champs Elysées and all the gentlemen are looking at you. Don't shuffle, Mademoiselle Adèle. Pick up your feet. Don't slouch. Don't waddle. Stop hugging me!

Much too plump for prettiness, Adèle. Fat babies charm, but fat girls do not. Adèle gobbled everything in sight, everything put in front of her. Despite the grim food sent up from that kitchen. The cook's idea of a treat for the upper servants was a slab of cold batter pudding, a roast onion, a tankard of beer. I used to creep downstairs in the night to the pantry larder and forage for the leftovers of Monsieur Rochester's dinner. A herb-scented wing of chicken, some shrimp tarts, a bunch of hothouse grapes, a slice of walnut cake. Into the dining-room I'd go, armed with Madam Fairfax's keys, filched from her pocket while she took forty winks, and help myself to the decanter of wine locked up in the sideboard.

For midnight feasts you want a companion but I had none. I couldn't let Adèle share in these secret meals. I've seen her scrape her little finger around an empty plate, forage for the fragment of lacy edge of omelette congealed there. I've watched her lick her little finger and press it onto the buttery crumbs of my finished toast then bring it up to her mouth. She was too greedy! I had to teach her self-control. She started bursting out of the satin frocks the master had had sent from Paris and I had to let them out at the seams. Together we looked at the pictures in Madam Fairfax's magazines: girls with proper hourglass figures. I shook my head at Adèle: she had no waist at all. Very soon we'd have to put her into a corset and see what we could achieve that way.

Bumping about in that huge house I felt very alone. I couldn't speak much English. The other servants thought I was odd, being a foreigner, and sniggered behind my back at what they called my parleyvoo, my peculiar ways. They hated French people because of the recent war. They thought we were heathens; savages; dangerous. Mademoiselle Eyre talked to me in half hour bursts, from time to time, in order to practise her French, but I could tell she didn't think much of me. I was a talking machine that was all. She practised on me as though I were a piano: thump thump thump with the loud pedal. She had no talent for the piano and very little for French. She feared and disliked the French, that was obvious. She had no feel for us, nor for our language. You can't speak a language well if you don't like the people you're addressing. *Oui, mademoiselle*, I would reply: *certainement, bien sûr.* In secret to myself I'd say and may the Blessed Virgin send you no children no health no happiness you cold-faced pudding-faced miseryguts.

Other people in that house were lonely too. Other people in that house were up and about at night. Monsieur Rochester went about his secret business, in and out of certain rooms, soundless as a spider. Often I watched him and he never knew. I found it hard to sleep, and in these restless moods I would pace the corridors, walking softly in my felt shoes, making no sound on the carpet of the first floor, the matting of the second. I didn't know what peace meant.

No peace for the wicked, the housekeeper used to say. Adèle wasn't wicked. The fire was an accident. I know she didn't mean to do it. It was Mademoiselle Eyre's fault for running away and leaving her. It was the fault of the lunatic girl.

So many sleepless people in that great house, taking their nightmares out for strolls. Footsteps creaked to and fro. Mademoiselle Eyre stole out of her room, a shawl over her nightgown. Over the matting she crept in her stockinged feet, her slippers clutched in her hand. Along the corridor she twinkled, popped into the master's bedroom. I saw her. Oh yes. I tiptoed after her. Sometimes it was the other way round and Monsieur Rochester visited her. He'd had her put in a room without bolt or key, so that she couldn't fence herself off from visitors. Tapping ever so quietly at her door, tap, tap, tap, and he vanished inside, while I hovered in the shadows unseen by either of them. I knelt down in the corridor and applied my eye to the keyhole. But the taper burnt too brightly in a dazzle of gold and the curtains of the bed were drawn so that I couldn't see anything.

The house came properly to life at night. That's when its true life began. All the words that couldn't be spoken in the daytime danced about in the shadows, darted about like bats flown in through an open window and knocking back and forth between the rafters. Bad words, which slithered down the polished staircase like snakes. Or they turned into sudden draughts of cold air which opened and slammed the doors, snuffed the candles, tickled the nape of your neck. I sat on my stool and crossed myself and prayed to the Holy Virgin. Help me. But we'd left the Holy Virgin far away, in France. She couldn't be a mother to us here.

Adèle's third mother was the lunatic girl. The Creole. She called Adèle *petite chérie*. She nuzzled at her like a cat licking its newborn.

I wish I could sleep. Yet I'm afraid to close my eyes and let darkness carry me away. I'm afraid of what I'll dream.

One night I dreamed I got up to search for Adèle. She

was missing from her bed. I tiptoed along the dark corridor. It seemed to go on and on for ever, like this train. A tunnel into endless night. Mr Rochester wasn't in his room. The governess's door was shut. I heard them laughing and I heard them rocking back and forth, gathering speed. Up the stairs I glided to the third storey. Moonlight stalked me through the pointed window. I saw Adèle. She'd got the mad girl with her. Both of them in their nightgowns; glimmering long and white. Their hair loose. Their feet bare. Adèle tugged the lunatic along the corridor. Now, *chérie*, walk nicely. Pick up your feet, don't shuffle. Shoulders back, chin up, can't you see the gentlemen are watching? Lift up your legs and dance for your papa then perhaps he'll give you a sugar lump. Lift up your legs and dance for the gentlemen and then perhaps they'll give you a bonbon especially if you let them peep up your skirts.

The lunatic copied her exactly. Pointed her fleshy toe and grinned, swayed ponderously from side to side. Two fat girls blundering along holding each other by the hand.

I took to tying Adèle into her bed at night. When she cried, I had to slap her. It's for your own good I screamed at her. I'm trying to keep you safe. Sleepwalkers come to mischief you little fool, they come to a bad end.

How did she get out? I'll never know. Again I tracked her, and again I found her in the company of the lunatic. By the open door Grace Poole snored in her easy chair.

The fire in the grate burnt low. In the chair opposite the naked madwoman had settled her bulk: her round belly, her meaty thighs. Not a day over twenty she looked. What a fresh, clear complexion: dark skin that gleamed gold. Caramel eyes. Her long black hair curled down to her waist. Too much hair. Thick and curly and black, tufts of it sprouting in her armpits as she raised her hand to scratch her head and yawned, a great nest of it at the base of her belly, between her legs. On her lap sprawled Adèle, twining her fingers in that torrent of hair and smiling while the madwoman crooned to her, embraced her and rocked her up and down, oh my little darling, my little pet, mamma's holding you, you're safe, you're safe. Adèle turned her face into the lunatic's breast, she nuzzled up to her, stroked that black hair looking soft as the feathers on her mother's cloak. The lunatic put her arms around her. She dandled Adèle just like a baby, kissed her with her big rosy mouth.

I ran back downstairs. I banged at the governess's door, I roused the housekeeper and the other servants, come quick come quick.

Later, we heard the madwoman weeping. Adèle, locked in her room, cried to match her.

In the morning Monsieur Rochester told us we had to go. Letting us go, he called it, as though we'd asked for it. Adèle was being packed off to boarding school far away, down in the south. The governess looked at her feet and smiled her prim little smile. But for all that she ran away soon after, and then there was the fire, and then Adèle and I caught this train.

Our final mother Adèle's and mine is this sleeper: a great lap which holds us securely as we doze and dream and remember a cradle lined with soft warm darkness which rocks us gently oh so gently back towards all we have lost her arms our true country our home.

Annunciation

Marie feels prepared for the angel when he whirrs into her life: used to strangers, keen for her to notice them, capering in front of her on the pavement, arms stretched wide. She doesn't tell her parents about these encounters. She protects them from knowing about the odd people out there, the men exposing themselves outside the school gates, or accosting her on her way home; burly toddlers whose catcalls beat on her shell like fists. Oyster-girl. She'd swallow anything, Marie, her classmates scoff. Open-mouthed and vulnerable and soft. That's the definition of a good girl in the early 1960s, and that's how the nuns in the grey stone convent school bring her up.

Slag or saint; you're allowed to choose. All to do with class. Bad girls, basically common, not respectable enough, from bad homes on the council estate, end up in the secondary modern along the road. They backcomb their hair, swagger and chew gum on the street, stroll home hatless, gossip about periods and pubic hair and French kissing, despise grammar and chant swear words instead, and under all the bravado accept the authorities' views of their utter worthlessness. Good girls like Marie, from good homes on the council estate, pass their eleven-plus and win scholarships to grammar school, have shiny noses and labour over their homework and get decent jobs.

Marie leaves school at eighteen, having failed her exams. She starts work as a clerk for the General Post Office on the Euston Road, in the addressograph office. Less of an office; more of a production line. The two older women she works with, Floss and Margaret, are resignedly kind, always ready to give a hand when Marie gets stuck or makes a mistake, but she doesn't know how to respond to the raucous banter they shout above the noise of the heavy machines. Pre-computer days, these: you punch letters and numbers onto metal printing plates. You can hammer the type and chainsmoke at the same time. Floss and Margaret keep the radio going all day long, plus a counterpoint flow of endless teasing. They bat saucy jokes back and forth, roaring when Marie doesn't get them. Hail Marie, full of gracelessness.

To celebrate her first pay-packet, Marie throws away the brown tweed skirt, yellow blouse and yellow cardigan she's worn at weekends for the past two years, buys a scarlet coat, a bright blue tartan shift dress, some white lace stockings and a black suspender belt, and a pair of white high-heeled plastic boots. She buys eyebrow tweezers, curlers, hair spray, a ladies' razor, pale beige foundation, pale pink lipstick, pale blue eyeshadow. No money left for food. For the next month she lives on sugar sandwiches; crunch of the sweet grains inside smears of cold marge glueing white bread slabs.

Now she needs a social life. She doesn't know how to make friends. Non-Catholics are frowned upon in her Catholic ghetto: iconoclast bullies who burst on Saturday afternoons out of their hunched brick church three streets away and march with noisy bands along the main road of the neighbourhood drumming angrily like a cloud of maddened hornets, marking out their territory; deluded heathens who eat sausages on Fridays, who refer to the Blessed Virgin simply as Mary and think she is just another woman.

Having no one to speak to, Marie writes in her diary: I enjoy being independent.

Her workmates shrug when she avoids the canteen at lunchtime. At night she ventures out on her own. Tricky going to the cinema, though. The moment the lights dim a man will arrive in the neighbouring seat and start to bother her, nudging and whispering, opening his flies. Eventually she has to get up and leave and miss the film. She doesn't complain to the manager. It's just how men are and you put up with it. The women at work, when she mentions it one coffee-break, say she should take it as a compliment: I should be so lucky! One day Floss reads a report of a rape in the newspaper: oooh I can't wait! They rock to and fro laughing.

Marie knows that good men exist. She feels certain that if she meets one she will recognise him immediately, because he'll treat her so well. She's willing to put up with being lonely while she waits, but in the interim she deals with men determined not to be lonely. When she walks around the city, men spring out at her from every crack and crevice, edging much too close, rubbing up against her, asking how much she charges. She realises it's because she's young, and on her own. She's got that wide-eyed look of the newcomer up from the suburbs and they're just trying their luck.

Other punters act more subtly, stepping up to her breezily convinced they've already met, smiling, asking the way somewhere. Asking the time. She lets some of these men steer her into a pub, buy her a drink, then take her back to their hotels. Salesmen. Her dad's job, that, before the war. Travellers in need of company, just like herself. She accepts that they just want a chat and feels daring going up to their rooms in the Bloomsbury back-streets. She lets one or two of them fuck her. It's what she's there for, isn't it: he buys her a gin and tonic, she drinks it, which shows she's willing. She doesn't know how to say no. She's been brought up to be accommodating and polite. Not to say boo to a goose. So you can't call it rape. Slag. She lies there and goes through the motions and feels nothing.

It's odd having sex with people you don't fancy, them lying over you slathering and groaning and jerking while you're not even liking their smell or the look of their prick, that mottled flobby thing they push into your hands and make you caress, and she doesn't like the slime of their come on her belly, either, cold like uncooked egg-white, and then afterwards the men turn on her and hate her for not having enjoyed herself. But it's all one in the eye for the parish priest and the nuns. Little whore, her father would call her if he knew; Dad who'd peep around her bedroom door and tease her: my eyes can see through walls! You're no child of mine! Mum shouts when she finds Marie aged ten reading Lolita. But Marie doesn't go home for Sunday lunch for a long time and so her parents don't find out she sleeps with men.

The psychiatrist her GP suggests she see, later on, during a bad patch in her early twenties, says: you pretend to be so innocent but you must have wanted it. Why deny that? Why can't you take some responsibility for what happened?

The round metal window behind his office chair forms his painted white halo; frame scarred with rust, peeling. The eyes of this mind-saint burn her up. Marie slumps on her orange vinyl chair. Mouth full of mud. She can't explain. He's like the parish priest. You don't talk back to that fiery judge.

The psychiatrist can't translate her mumblings. He repeats: you seek out situations of seduction. Marie wonders: so that's what it's called.

After a while she learns to keep her eyes down in the

street, and not to look around her; so fewer men try it on. Giving up on cinema she goes to evening classes instead: art history, watercolour painting, dressmaking. Then she comes home, quite cheerful, to her bedsit in Earl's Court.

At the time of meeting Joe, the angel, she's just begun renting a flat in Museum Street with three of the girls from work. An old mansion block. Kitchenette, lounge, four beds in one room, bathroom on the floor below. You can't bring a boyfriend back to spend the night because there's no privacy. You have to make other arrangements.

One Saturday her three flatmates decide to hold a party. Marie has been there a month. She stays and watches the proceedings for a while because she doesn't know what else to do or where else to go. She feels safer indoors than braving the streets on her own. She knocks back a few halves of cider, and then it's easy just to flop on a brown velvet floor cushion and pretend nothing unusual is happening.

Four men, fellow clerks from work, arrive. People she knows well enough to say hello to. They push the furniture out of the way and roll back the mustard nylon carpet. They take the tattered armchairs and the formica-topped coffee table into the bedroom, upend the crimson velvet settee, and put down beanbags for sitting on.

At first Marie assumes it's going to be a normal Saturday night party. Her flatmates giggle in the corners, finessing their plans, and she shrugs. She's been to one or two parties by now: lights switched off; groping in the dark and yelping; Marie perching primly on the arm of a chair feeling stupid. This lot are all chatting and joshing each other just as they do at work. They carry in a case of beer, pour peanuts and Twiglets into saucers, arrange ashtrays.

Then her flatmates suspend black sheets from the walls, lay a black sheet on the floor, and light the room with black candles. They invert a crucifix and prop it up over the fireplace, place a plastic skull, such as you buy in joke shops, on the mantelpiece, and pin up a tatty poster of a goat. Marie does not feel at all outraged. She just feels she's in a cold, ashy place. It's like sitting in an empty grate. She realises she doesn't believe in God any more. There's no God to be offended by what this lot are getting up to. They simply want to feel daring and wicked. The satanic decorations are just a way of spicing things up.

Marie in her blue tartan mini-dress sits fiddling with the idea of the loss of God. Her flatmates and the four male clerks burn joss-sticks and play rock music and pass joints around and sling down the beer. Marie curls up by the record-player and tries to become invisible.

Eventually the others start dancing and taking their clothes off at the same time. All those white bums and white penises joggling around; those curly-haired triangles masking those cunts. Such soft bodies. Stripped of their workaday clothes, their party costumes, how impersonal but how vulnerable they look. The room smells of dust. How intimate the sweaty dimness. Marie riffles through the record collection, clutches a Dylan album, pretends to read the sleeve. Peers at the print but can't make out a word.

Next comes a bit of mucking about with the crucifix, the men stroking each other with it, taking turns sliding its stem into the girls' fannies. When her three flatmates sort themselves out a partner each, and lie down on the floor and begin having sex, Marie feels in the way. Also she realises that the fourth man is making his way across the room towards her.

She's sitting there, isn't she? That's what the psychiatrist points out. So she's joined in.

Sort of. She doesn't know how to leave. She lives there, after all. But where can she go? What should she do? Sit in the bathroom downstairs all night? The bedroom's crammed with the sitting-room furniture and the kitchenette has no door. She feels stuck, heavy, as though she's been drugged. Don't make a fuss. The flat seems so different with the lights turned off, the curtains safety-pinned together; just the glow of the candles on the mantelpiece. Everyday life has been smoothed away and in its place has come a great nothingness. The blackness and the blankness of the room snuff out the wriggling white bodies on the floor, as though they're dead. Nothing matters and no one has given Marie permission to leave and in the morning everyone will laugh at her for not enjoying herself. They won't tell Floss, though, or Margaret, when they go back to work after the weekend, about the goings-on. Those two would really draw the line at such antics. They won't approve of capering about in your birthday suit and making mock.

Marie wishes it were indeed Monday morning and she were leaving for work to be teased by Floss for naïveté and to hear Margaret complain about her daughter-in-law. So she decides to make morning happen. She makes an enormous effort. Although she's as heavy as a mountain she finds willpower from somewhere. She manages to get up, avoid her would-be swain's clutch, stumble out. Handbag clutched under her arm she bumps down the stairs and into the street.

If she keeps running she won't meet anyone and then there'll be no trouble. But she's wearing stilettos and she trips and falls into a puddle. She sprawls on the pavement, her knees smarting and stinging, and starts crying.

Enter the angel. Joe, whistling, turns the corner and finds her. What's this? What's this? Sweetie. Oh you poor thing. He helps her up, holds her arm gently, walks her down Charing Cross Road, then right into Old Compton Street.

The West End blazes with light. How astonishing: evening still dances and frolics: not the middle of the night at all. London isn't ashy dead asleep but very much alive and shining, and the Soho pubs stand open-doored, and inside them men sit around smoking and reading the evening paper in the most normal of ways, having a quiet pint and doing the crossword before going off to meet their girlfriends. They all have friends, Marie feels sure; they don't need to badger girls, they like girls but they're not desperate. Take it or leave it. And they go back to the sports pages. That's so comforting. She can stroll in here with Joe and no one will bother her.

Joe eases her through the pub, hand steering her elbow. She sits down with him in the mirror-walled saloon bar; they tuck themselves into the curve of a leather bench in a dim corner. Joe makes Marie take off her shoes. He crouches in front of her, dabs at her grazed knees, scarlet-pink under torn nylon, dries her wet stockinged feet with his blue handkerchief patterned with yellow paisley squiggles. He apologises for the brown stain on one corner: I was mopping up some spilt chemicals. Smiling at his apology and obviously not meaning one word of it. Cocking an eyebrow at her to see what she makes of him.

Thank you, she begins.

He holds up one long forefinger. Just like the angel on Christmas cards. He's got a creased, reddish, battered-looking face, thinning curly fair hair that flies up round his head. He buys Marie a gin and tonic. Just tell me what happened, babe.

She blurts something out, and he begins laughing, as though she's actually quite dashing and witty, despite her laddered stockings and her broken heel and her tears. He coaxes it out of her. So what's the matter, then? She tells him her sorry tale and he starts laughing again.

You're mocking me, Marie sobs.

No, Joe says: it's the poster of the goat that's funny, not you.

He doesn't try and come on to her in any way. So she starts to like him, that quickly. She's grateful to him.

She swallows down her second gin and tonic.

Oh, I do love gin, she says.

Sharpness cut with sweetness, the bubbles of the tonic fizzing up her nose, the ice clinking against the sides of the glass, the frosted lemon slice. She smokes one of Joe's cigarettes. After a third gin and tonic she feels cheerier. Her feet lose their numbness now that her stockinged toes are drying out in the warmth. Her face feels rosy again and when she checks in her compact mirror her melted mascara hasn't made her too much of a panda.

Joe's been to an opening in Cork Street and is on his way home. Marie doesn't know what an opening is but she nods and pretends she does. She brightens up, begins to feel she belongs in the world, watches herself in the engraved glass mirror opposite, powdering her nose and applying fresh lipstick. She starts enjoying the noise of jukebox music and chatter and the acrid smell of fag smoke. She comes back to life because she's got someone to talk to. She tells him all about her evening classes.

Back in the street she halts in a doorway, stands on one foot and then on the other to peel off her stockings, throws her bunched stockings and her broken shoes into the gutter. Arm in arm with Joe she pads away barefoot. Joe buys fish and chips then hails a taxi and takes her back to his place. Only one bed: Marie shares it with him. He doesn't try anything on. She can't believe it: how nice, how respectful he is.

Sunday morning he digs her out a pair of plum velvet stilettos from the back of a cupboard, old ones his ex-girlfriend's left behind, brews tea, grills kippers and toast, goes out for the papers. Sunday lunchtime they go to another Soho pub, a different one from the night before, and drink Bloody Marys. Joe points out the silvery urn on the counter which dispenses water into your shot of pastis, clouds the sherbet-yellow to pale lemon.

A French drink. You want to try it?

Marie sips pastis, tickled by its aniseed taste. Sweeties. She smiles at the people pressing in on all sides. She's become part of the crowd. Lots of the men in here know Joe. They dig him in the ribs and call him you old dog. Several of them insist on kissing her hand. Then Joe escorts Marie to her flat. Having him with her makes her feel bold. She doesn't have to explain anything, just hands over a week's rent in lieu of notice. She packs her stuff. At Joe's she cooks supper: eggs and bacon and black pudding.

Monday she goes into work as usual. Her ex-flatmates

don't say anything in front of Floss and Margaret and neither does she. In the evening she goes back to Joe's. An address near Mornington Crescent tube. A half-converted warehouse, which he shares with two other photographers. He's on the ground floor and they're above. Walls of bare brick; an interior dedicated to photography, to the clutter and paraphernalia of work. Marie considers the smell of chemicals, the oil heater fumes, the untidiness, romantic and glamorous. A mattress on a platform forms Joe's bed, and the bathroom doubles as the galley kitchen. You clean your teeth in the kitchen sink and heave a board over the bath and then you can stack the washing-up on it. A cold-water sink, a small hanging larder for food, a two-ring Baby Belling, all packed in tight together. The cement-floored lavatory out the back, at the side of the yard, smells of damp wood. Invisible trains clank and rattle over nearby railway lines, in and out of Euston.

No accident, is it, Marie's falling in with Joe, toeing his line. The psychiatrist points that out. Though she's taken by surprise she helps to bring about her fall. She consents. She jumps into the free air and he catches her. One reason for her continuing obsession with him: he catches her and knows her. Sees right through her. Sees her for who she truly is. Tells her what he sees.

Stupid girl, he says to her fondly: stupid girl.

He finds her out. He recognises her fear. He sniffs it, forces her to confess to it. She can't fool him. The first time he wants sex with her she doesn't come. He fingers her too abruptly, impatient for her to heat up and be ready. Instead she gets jumpy and irritable. He rubs her too hard. When's this going to stop? Can't he just get on with it, enter her, fuck her, pant and gasp, flop on top of her, fall asleep? By now Marie does know how to make men come: you move your hips in a certain way and that does for them; then they leave you alone.

In Joe's copy of *Lady Chatterley's Lover*, the gamekeeper Mellors says doing that is a proof of hating men. Marie does think some of them are disgusting. She thinks she's disgusting too, letting any of them come near her. She's had that well drummed into her at school; and sometimes she thinks her parents were right; she doesn't like those swollen cocks, as she explains to the psychiatrist, which have a life of their own and seem to have little to do with the human beings they're attached to; there are far too many cocks in the world always popping out of men's trousers just when you're longing for a bit of peace, and she hates being nagged for not enjoying herself more.

The psychiatrist agrees with the gamekeeper Mellors: Marie is promiscuous and frigid; she hates men and wants to castrate them. She's faking it: pretending to be so innocent but really wanting to bite men's penises off.

Long before she meets Joe, Marie does indeed learn to fake it, because that helps shorten the whole experience and also you don't get told off for failing to come. She tries to fake it with Joe but he knows what she's up to and laughs. He knows she fakes her orgasms because she fakes so badly. He gets the power over her that way, knowing she's lied, knowing she can't come, then showing her how to.

The trouble with you, darling, you've got to be forced to enjoy yourself. Oh, you Catholics.

He ties her up. He knots Marie's hands and feet to the bedstead with silk scarves. He touches and rubs her, gently now, taking his time, until she comes. Then he photographs her. Then he fucks her. Then he photographs her again. Then he unties her. Sometimes he doesn't fuck her at all, just ties her up and photographs her splayed legs. Gorgeous, darling: gorgeous. Sometimes he dresses her up: lipsticked nun flashing her knickers; pouting little First Communicant shedding her dress, her veil. Marie feels taken care of; as though Joe's her mother, the scarves her mother holding her. Silky hands saying come on darling this is for your own good. Rapture of surrender to those hands, to those eyes, to that camera. Rapture of giving Joe everything he asks for: her attention, her love, her cries.

Not just sadistic and promiscuous but masochistic as well, explains the psychiatrist, peering at her over his spectacles. Marie struggles for words.

She calls Joe the pirate. She lets Joe do it. Become bad Joe, bullying her, who turns back into good Joe, kissing her, overcome with remorse. She stays with him. Every night she goes back to him for more.

Why? Well, you see, she stumbles: I mattered to him. He loved me and he needed me.

Good Joe, good little boy Joe, tells her about his past, and she passionately and compassionately understands him, his hard childhood, the loss of his mother who agrees with his father to banish him to prep school aged only seven. His mother didn't fight to keep him at home. As a result he lost all faith and trust in her. That's why he's difficult, Marie knows: that's why he sometimes loses his temper and turns into bad Joe who slaps her. He slaps her: she's a slapper. Good Joe, the angel, takes her hand at table, holds it and beams at her, calls her darling, sweetie, babe, loves to cuddle and kiss, worships women his muses. Good Joe forgets bad Joe, the devil with blinking camera-red eyes, who claims women as fellow devils: they've let him down over and over again, hurt him, abandoned him. Marie will never hurt Joe or let him down or abandon him. With her love she will rescue him and mend him and make him happy and then he'll never need to hit her again. Or tie her up for that matter.

Marie learns what not to say or do, to keep out of his way when he's in one of his moods, not to interrupt him when he's talking to people at openings or in the pub. At least he's got feelings. He isn't cold and distant. He was easily hurt, she tells the psychiatrist: very sensitive to slights, but he was lovely company, in the main. He had a soul, and he made me feel I had one too.

Joe has to go and see his wife sometimes. He makes

that clear from the start. When Marie comes back in the evening from her job he's sometimes there and sometimes not. She always cooks, in case he comes in. These nights when she's by herself she drinks a bottle of beer and reads. She's given up her evening classes, which don't fit with being available for Joe, but she still wants to improve herself. She goes to the public library and borrows books by D. H. Lawrence, Albert Camus, T. S. Eliot, Colette, the Brontës. On Saturday afternoons, if Joe's out visiting his family, she rummages in the second-hand bookshops on the Charing Cross Road and comes home with a bagful of bargains. Or she rummages through the bookstalls near the market on Inverness Street, where she shops for vegetables and meat. Cheap cuts like breast of lamb, ends of bacon joints, pie veal, eked out with potatoes or rice. When money's more plentiful she makes fancy peasant dishes she's never previously heard of but which now, with a copy of Marguerite Patten propped open, she learns to cook: boeuf Stroganoff, stuffed green peppers, chilli con carne, moussaka.

She accompanies Joe to shows, dressing up for him in her new outfits. She buys a skinny mini dress in purple and another in orange paisley, with a low scoop neck. She buys a white jersey tunic and matching trousers, cut very lean. Tight armholes on the long tight sleeves, edged with white cloth-covered buttons, which finish in points coming down over the backs of your hands. The same buttons on the flyfront. She buys new makeup too: pale face powder, dark sludgy eyeshadow, vampy lipstick. False eyelashes and false fingernails.

She parades for Joe in the purple mini dress, showing off her long legs and her newly blonde hair.

Beautiful chick, says Joe.

Marie stares at herself in the mirror, to find her beauty.

A perfectly calm and blank face; big eyes giving nothing away; a mouth that does not talk. Does beauty come from gleaming cheekbones, full lips? She's not sure. She's not certain that her beauty is hers. She lives just behind her beauty. Nobody knows what she's really like. That's her fault, because she doesn't tell them. She can't talk to any of Joe's friends because they're all so brilliant, artists and photographers; she never knows what to say. They don't want to talk to her, in any case. She's Joe's floosie. It's not her place, to be talked to. She models for some of them, as well as for Joe. Those of his painter friends who've gone on producing figurative work rather than abstract. They shout at each other about this all the time in the pub; sometimes they get into fights, lug each other out onto the street where there's more space for punch-ups. Marie often gets drunk too, then has a hangover next day, turns up late to work. In the end, when the supervisor threatens her with the sack, she just walks out. She doesn't say a proper goodbye to Floss and Margaret. She just goes. She drinks too much in the pub that night and ends up crying.

Floosie-woozy, says Joe.

They're in a pickle now because money is so short. Marie begins modelling in art school life-classes part-time, and gets a waitressing job three days a week in a coffee-bar.

From time to time Joe gets a good commission, or sells prints in between shows. He chats up the punters who drift into the gallery, stays in touch with them, then invites them round. Rich women trailing husbands with chequebooks. They adore visiting a real studio, discovering the stacks of canvases in racks. Oh Joe, why don't you go on painting? they coo. One woman called Anne has bought three of Joe's prints. He takes Marie with him to deliver them and pick up the cheque. Anne lives in a large shabby villa in Notting Hill. She's got the same name, almost, as Marie's mother, but she doesn't resemble her. She's old enough to be a grandmother but she doesn't look like one. Dyed black hair in a Louise Brooks bob, short black silk dress, fabulous legs, high heels. She screeches with laughter and calls Joe and Marie darling.

At first Marie feels nervous, even though by now she knows not to hold a knife like a pencil, and to say lavatory, sofa, napkin, and so on. If she were a proper Cockney she'd be presentably quaint, but lower-middle-class is just drab. Another reason to keep her mouth shut in company and just look beautiful. Upper-class people spot you instantly, whether you keep your mouth shut or not. Anne sees through Marie's languid pose immediately.

Marie watches her sizing her up. Then she feels her being nice. She draws Marie into the conversation, not with that kind of pretend politeness that is like a slap round the face, terribly condescending, but as though she likes her.

They sit in a white drawing-room, furnished with antique mirrors, fat white cushions on the white sofas, big modern pictures on the walls. Marie hardly dares breathe in case she dirties something.

Come on, darling, Anne says: have another glass of bubbly.

They drink two bottles of champagne. Anne writes Joe his cheque.

I'll give one of these to my god-daughter Lizzie. She's living in some funny little place in the East End. Could do with some brightening up.

Joe burps and gets up. He jerks his head at Marie: time to be off.

In the doorway Anne puts her hand on Joe's arm, looks him in the eye. She says: now just make sure you're kind to that little girl and don't do anything to hurt her.

Marie realises: she means me.

She wants to hurl herself at Anne; she wants to sit in the armchair with her and feel her arms around her; she wants to lie in her lap like a baby; she fears she'll start crying and never stop.

Head down, she hurries out after Joe and doesn't even say goodbye to her kind hostess, let alone thank her for the champagne. Out in the street Joe gives her a quick slap for her bad manners. You've got to learn! Then he takes her out for a Chinese meal.

Lots about Joe that Marie doesn't know, even though she rifles through his things when he's out, reads any letter he leaves lying around, attempts to listen to his conversations on the telephone. She does discover that, contrary to what he's told her, he's divorced, and his children grown-up. He doesn't want Marie to meet his kids. He's kept her away from them. She has assumed their love affair has had to be kept a secret because his kids are so young.

Now she dares to ask him: so where do you go, then, on the nights you're not with me?

Good Joe digs his hands into his trouser pockets, says: come on babe. She's standing at the stove, frying chips. When he does not reply she swivels and looks him in the eye.

Go on, tell me. Where d'you go?

Now you're beginning to sound like my wife, he says: OK, my ex-wife. I love you because you never nag or whinge. Don't spoil it.

Marie turns back to the chips seething in their bath. Joe comes up behind her, puts his arms around her, pinches her nipples. Marie gasps and stiffens. He pinches harder. She doesn't dare wriggle out of his embrace lest in the struggle the pan tilts over and boiling fat splashes all over her and onto the gas flame.

Tell me you're only joking, bad Joe says, pincering her breasts.

The following evening Marie gets pissed at an opening and allows one of Joe's mates to chat her up. She and Joe have a row in the street. Back at home he gives her a smack in the face. Then he goes out to fetch them some fish and chips. Good Joe bad Joe good Joe bad Joe the images flicker very fast and begin to cohere into just one Joe who'll hit her kiss her hit her kiss her and perhaps should be left. But where can she go? That's the problem. Think about it, Marie tells herself. Next morning, wearing dark glasses to hide her black eye, she goes as usual to her waitressing job at the coffee bar on Oxford Street.

Soon afterwards she discovers she's pregnant.

How could you have let it happen? asks the psychiatrist: that was careless, wasn't it? You'd found out he was divorced. Perhaps you hoped he'd marry you?

Marie goes to Joe's GP, who points out abortion is illegal and scolds her for even considering one. You're young and healthy: you should be ashamed of yourself.

He sits twiddling his fountain pen while Marie wriggles her soggy handkerchief out of her sleeve and blows her nose.

Marie tells Joe the news that evening. Before supper. She has forgotten to buy any fresh food so he is already resentful. Baked beans yet again. She positions herself near the kitchen door and eyes him fearfully. You'll have to get rid of it, he says: sorry, but there we are. I don't want another kid. Marie says: but I don't know how to get an abortion. Joe begins shouting. She scuttles out into the back yard, into the lavatory, shoots the bolt. She'll wait here until he has stormed off to the pub. She leans against the door, rubbing her cheek on the rough towel hanging there. The towel dries her tears. Towel of tenderness, mopping her. Frayed towel worn into holes, valiantly absorbing her wet despite its thinness. Towel, towel, tell me what to do. Oh towel comfort me.

Crash of the street door. Quietness. She closes the lid of the lavatory, sinks down onto it, warm wooden seat, tears off a piece of lavatory paper and starts to play with it, strokes her fingers up and down over its cool, smooth surface. She yanks at it, tears it into little bits in her lap. What was that game with the flower petals you ripped off? He loves me he loves me not. I'll have a baby no I'll not. How can I possibly become a mother? It wouldn't be fair on the child. Poor little tyke.

She can't ring her parents and ask for help. To them abortion is a mortal sin. Herod's Slaughter of the Innocents all over again, punished by an eternity in hellfire. She has lost touch with her former flatmates and good riddance. She feels too ashamed to contact Floss and Margaret, tell them what's happened, ask for advice. She's got no friends. Stupid girl, she berates herself: stupid girl.

She crosses the yard, tests the back door. Good. Joe hasn't locked her out. Inside the studio she picks up the fallen chair, kicks the bits of smashed tea cup under the table, then goes back into the kitchen and collects up pound notes from where she's stashed them in various hiding-places: under the coal-scuttle, behind the fridge, at the back of a stack of plates. Her lump sums for the shopping, the launderette, the rent. She empties the jam jar of money for feeding the electricity and gas meters. Joe's cleared the saucerful of beer money. But he's left his overcoat behind. Her fingers steal through his pockets and add his loose change to the bulk in her purse. Enough to see her through the next couple of days.

Hastily she packs a bag with her clothes, a clutch of books. Bag, you're my friend. Come with me now. She dons a chiffon headscarf, her white plastic raincoat, and slips out, walks south into the darkness humming with cars. Few passersby. Cheer up, darling, the men call after her, but she hardly notices them. She's just a shadow among other shadows. She can lose herself here, hide in these impersonal streets. She can fade away and not be visible to anyone.

She ducks past pubs where Joe may be drinking. Walking in high heels, lugging a bag heavy with books, means she doesn't get very far. She blunders along, not sure at first where to go. She turns east onto the Euston Road, blackness glistening with rain and headlights, with a vague idea of finding a backstreet route down into southern Bloomsbury, the places she remembers around

Museum Street. No. She doesn't belong there any more. Stick to the Euston Road. Make towards the Angel. Joe was the angel. Tears spring out on her face.

Arms and feet aching, she gives up at Kings Cross. She turns her face southwards, decides to try the first cheap-looking hotel she can see. On the Grays Inn Road, she halts at a pub, goes into the off-licence, buys a bottle of beer. She coaxes the barman to sell her the staling cheese roll, thin tongue of sweaty cheddar lolling between hard white lips, left over from lunch, which sits under a Perspex dome on the counter of the public bar. She packs beer and cheese roll into her handbag and returns to the street. A little further along she spots a suitably shabby brown front. Sign propped in the window spells out Vacancies. In she goes over the dimpled nylon mat. She takes a room for the night, hauls herself up the steep, narrow stairs. She shuts and locks the door. Turns round to survey her space.

Brown walls. Brown lino floor. Cracked wash hand basin with a small mirror tilting above it. Naked light bulb casts a pool of dingy yellow. Someone's been round with a mop soaked in disinfectant: the room smells cold and clean.

Marie edges in. At first she hardly dares breathe: the air presses her flat as a flower in blotting-paper between two books. The air sticks her in place, a deckle-edged photo of a nice child in a family album, caught in transparent photo corners. Nobody else can see these discreet triangles and so they assume she's free to move but she's not. The air grips her, holds her tight. She must fight the air, push her hands into it, beat at it, swing it off her. She must be courageous, open her mouth, learn to scream.

She doesn't need to scream. She's by herself. Safe. She can breathe out. She can co-habit with the space, bring it towards her, feel it lightly against her skin. Cool, dusty air. Push and pull of Marie within the space, leaning on the air, feeling it lean back on her like a friendly animal. She can move in the space. She can test out the distance between sink and bed, between wardrobe and chair. She can reach out and switch on the lamp beside the bed. She can decide whether or not she likes the grubby white pleats of its shade, its brown frayed flex. No audience: that's the whole point. No one watching her or telling her what to do or pushing her out of the way or lunging at her. The chair doesn't grab her. The bed doesn't shout fuck. The wardrobe waits for her to approach and ask it to open up. The overhead bulb doesn't swing against her face, a scorching fist. The walls don't catch her in a crushing embrace.

She walks into the centre of the room, drops her bag and handbag. Her coat loafs away and hangs itself on the back of the door. Her shoes kick off to the far corner. Her bag yawns. Her handbag unsnaps its mouth and bids her a vinyl welcome.

She arranges her chorus-line of decorous couples –

comb and brush, toothpaste and toothbrush, flannel and soap – on the veneer-top stool. They line up together and don't squabble. She lays out her collection of books on the striped rag rug next to the bed. They lie like obedient children in a hospital ward. She changes her mind, changes the books into building blocks, stacks them into a wobbly pile, pushes it over. Like a girl falling down, a ruffle of paper covers, paper frilled skirts. She drapes her chiffon scarf over the orange plush chair to hide its scarred arms. She strokes the scarf into place: there you are, chair, no one will burn you with cigarettes now, I've tucked you up with this soft bandage so you'll feel all right.

Sobs want to heave up, like water glug-glugging deep in the waste-pipe under the basin, under the floorboards. How noisy that sink wants to be. Sobs remain a distant music, part of the murmur of traffic outside, the radio playing skiffle in the room next door.

The jumpy furniture, soothed now, settles down around her. She flattens the hiccuping rug with her foot, seats herself experimentally on the narrow single bed, pats it. Hard. Good, says schoolmistress Marie. Unyielding mattress won't let her sink into self-pity, will bear her up all night across that ocean of tears congealed to brown lino. She sits cross-legged on the worn orange chenille coverlet and chews the stale cheese roll, swigs from the bottle of beer. She lights a cigarette. Inhale and exhale; kiss and spit; she's got a relationship. She consumes the nicotine. She keeps it company. Don't go, cigarette, don't go. She stubs it out, lights another. From her toppled heap of books she selects a novel by Jean Rhys.

Marie leans on one elbow. Soft ridges of chenille press back at her. The book in her hand is alive and speaks to her. Lying here with the book, it's as though the book is another body close to hers, the book reaches out and touches Marie on the shoulder, taps her and says listen, you can get the money, easy, just charge men for sex. The book draws her into an embrace, settles back, twines her legs around her, strokes her towards sleep, towards dreams.

In the morning she washes in cold water, goes out for a cup of tea in the next-door café. Good thing she scribbled down Anne's surname and address while they were still fresh in her memory, brought the screwed-up piece of paper with her. The public phone booth smells of urine. She holds the heavy door open with one foot, swings up the directory from underneath the phone, looks up Anne's number. She fishes out four pennies from her purse, dials the number. Oh baby, Anne says.

Anne drives Marie over to the place where her god-daughter Lizzie lives in Stepney. Decaying Victorian house, rented from a local landlord. Full of girls. Art students, teachers, librarians. Men come and go, but it's the girls' house.

Lizzie says: there's a room going spare. You're welcome.

Marie moves in.

She gives birth the following December, at the London Hospital. Once the baby is brought home the household throws a party in the kitchen, to bless and welcome him. They encircle his head with a wreath of tinsel and evergreen, hang strings of lights above his basket, light candles, splash drops of gin and tonic on his brow, sing to him. Marie lights a cigarette and looks on, amused. At least they like a drink. Today they're catering for all tastes. Beer and cider, gin, a bottle of Veuve du Vernay.

When she remembers to, Lizzie helps Marie in her cheerful, slapdash way. She takes the baby out for an airing, to give Marie a chance to catch up on her sleep, helps her fill in forms for the DHSS, soaks nappies in buckets.

Sometimes, when the baby wakes at three or four a.m. and cries for a feed, Lizzie hears him. She creeps out of her own room, peeps round Marie's door. Marie, still half asleep, pulling a blanket around her shoulders, fumbling to fit the baby to her breast, looks up and nods: come in. Lizzie, wrapped in a second blanket, perches on the end of the bed in the darkness. Then gradually she sprawls across the eiderdown, propped on one elbow. Sometimes they chat; exchange confidences. Sometimes they remain in silence. Cold air blows in from the gap at the top of the ill-fitting sash window, rattle of a far away train, murmur of lorries on a distant road. The room holds them. The baby gulps and burps. They swim in an ordinariness that feels safe, that lets their edges blur and loosen. Sometimes they roll up the paper blind so that they can see the moon through the black glass. Smell of warm cotton, clean nappies airing in front of the gas fire, and milk. The three of them sit peacefully together, part of the London night.

The Lay of Bee Wolf

Long time back, long long time, in a land of rock, mud, swamp, bog, fog, mist, and rain, men had to be tough if they were to live. A man who was a milk sop, who did not like to fight, would die young. A beast would eat him. Or a wild man would kill him. You had to be in a gang to be safe. You had to have a lord on top. Each lord chose his squad of men. Great love each felt for each: hey, bro, let me take care of you. If you met a strange squad, a strange gang, on your own turf, then you felt rage: how dare they come in to my space? What cheek! So then the lords of the gangs would shout: war! So they would go to war. Men fought men. Much death. Wounds and blood. Much gold, too. That was the point of all those wars: if you won them you could grab the gold. So the pain of the fight and the fear of death was worth it: you might grab the gold. Then your lord would be king of a new land and he would get a lot of new slave girls to fuck and he would dig holes at the back of caves to hide the gold in: his fine gold hoard.

Each gang had a hall: a low house with a hole in the roof to let out the smoke of the fire. At night the men came back from their wars to these long huts, their halls, where they lay down on fur rugs, and their wives came to them with soap and soft cloths, to give them a wash, and a back rub, and then gave them good things to eat such as roast deer or roast ox or roast duck, and then the men drank a great deal of beer and mead and got drunk and took up their harps and sang songs to help them get their hearts back, to help them get through the huge fear they all felt of the dark and of death. Life, they sang, was like a lit hall. Dark all round it. A man was like a small bird: by chance he flew in to the warm lit hall, for a space, then left it, went back once more out to the cold dark, which was death.

Let me tell you a tale of one great lord. His name was Bee Wolf. For his close chums just Bee. He wore a skin coat made from all the wild beasts he slew: a strip off each. His boots, made of dead seals, had soles of wood. He had stag horns on his hat and a big round shield with a big boss, plus a spear with a sharp point. At night he would lay down sword, spear and shield, take off his fur coat and boots, loll in a robe (as all the chaps did), take up his harp, and sing songs. He would pluck a song from his word hoard and give it his best.

Bee was fond of his wife and of his three girls. He would chat to them, and write songs for them, and bring them to sit near him on wood stools round the fire at night. He gave his wife a gold belt set with gems and a gold band for her hair. He taught his girls to sing and to play the harp. He slept with his wife in a wood bed at the far end of the hall, with his girls near by. He was a lord, so he had a bed with a fur rug on it. All the rest of his folk slept on mats.

Bee taught his wife and girls to fight. He gave each one a spear and a sword and a shield. Come on, he would shout: just have a go! In time they were quite good at it. You do not know, said Bee to his male chums: the day may come when girls need to know how to fight. The day may come when girls will want and need to be part of a gang. Just you wait and see.

One night a great beast, a sort of huge worm, a bit like a fat snake on short legs, with scales on its back and sharp claws, slunk in from the far off wild, from that dark place of swamps and mists, as foul as hell, that bad land that men fear so much, and crept to the hall on paws of slime. The guards at the door had gone to sleep, drunk. They woke in a start of fear to find a beast nose to nose with them.

In fact the beast had gone out to play, got lost, and then, when night fell, could not find the way home. It blew flames through its mouth to light up the dark so that it could see. But in the dark all paths seem the same. So the beast was well lost.

Please help me, said the beast to the guards in beast talk: I have got lost and do not know my way. Please would you point out the way home? And I need some food or I will die. I feel so weak. Please help me.

The guards could not know what the beast said. They just saw the flames and the slime on the paws and the scales and the great jaws and the sharp teeth. Full of fear, they gave a scream. Oh, said the beast. The guards heard what they thought was a fierce snarl and so they gave a fresh scream. A vile beast! Quick! Kill it! Swords and spears out, they did their best to kill it. So then, full of rage, with one snap of its teeth the beast ate them up, plus most of the men who slept, drunk, on their mats near the door. Too late for them to fight. They were beast snacks. Off went the beast, with a bit of a limp, blood on its jaws.

Bee, in bed with his wife, woke up and said to her: I think I have had a bad dream. May I tell it to you?

No time for that, I fear, she said: I heard a noise and I want to go and see what made it.

Bee said: all right, love, and then come back here and I will make us a nice cup of mead and then you can tell me what is up.

His wife went to look. Oh oh. Not good news.

The next night the beast came back. Still lost, it still sought its way home. It cried out once more in beast words: please help me.

You see this vile beast? cried the guards to Bee. Bee knew that as lord of the gang he had to look brave for his men. In fact he did not much like to fight at all. He did not want to die. He gave a sigh: all right then. If I must.

So Bee and the few men left to him, plus his wife, and their girls, all fought the beast. Knee deep in blood, they cut off its head, tail, cock, paws. With a last thrash and snarl, in a stench of slit gut, gas, slime and shit, the huge beast died.

Let us rip off its skin, said Bee: and then at least I will get a new coat out of all this mess.

He tore off the skin. At the back, at the neck, he found a name tape, such as you would stitch on a coat for a small child off to school for the first time. The name of the beast, done in red print on the name tape, was Gren Dell. The wife of Bee took a look. Hmmm, said she. That is neat work. Hem stitch. A beast that can sew! Hmmm.

That night they held a feast. Bee put on his new skin coat. A good fit. He and his wife and girls and the few men left to them drank a great deal, made up new songs of praise, drank toasts, spoke boasts. Bee was too drunk to get to bed with his wife. His girls went to sleep near her, on their mats. Bee fell to sleep by the fire. Two guards sat near the door. Just in case. But they were drunk, too, and full of sleep.

From far off in the wild, from the place of swamps and mists, came a roar. Out of the dark came a huge beast. Far more huge than the first beast.

Who was this beast? She was Ms Dell, the mum of Gren, of course. She came to look for her son. He had not come home for the last two nights. She gave a call from deep in her heart. Son, son, time to come home! You might meet a strange man and then you might get hurt! Son, son, come home to your mum! Oh my dear one, where are you? Oh my sweet boy, hear me call your name!

The hall guards slept. Snore snore snore. In crept Ms Dell on tip toe. Tip claw, I should say. She saw Bee. He slept by the fire in his new coat of skin. His beast coat. He had the smell of Gren, the look of Gren. So of course the mum of Gren thought this was Gren. She thought she had found her son, her wee boy who had got lost. How glad she felt! Oh my babe, my dear babe, my sweet one, she cried. With a big smile and a quick snap of her jaws she had him. She held him by the scruff of his neck. He still slept, her wee man-cub. A snore like a purr. With a lash of her long tail she was gone. She bore him off with her. She took him home.

Dawn broke. The wife of Bee, and his girls, could not find him. Not in his bed, not by the fire. They made a loud cry: oh woe oh woe. They wept. Their lord was gone. So were the few men and the two guards they thought still left to them. No, those men had all run off, to find a new gang, a strong new lord. So that he would trust them they would tell him where he could find gold, a fine hall full of furs and harps, and girls to fuck. Then, the fuck done, the new lord might just kill them. The wife and her girls would die in great fear and great pain.

The wife and her girls were on their own. All too soon,

they were sure, that new strange lord would come with his gang, steal their gold, take them off as slaves, fuck them then kill them. True, they had arms, and could fight, but they were but one wife and three girls – too few to win a war. Oh woe oh woe.

They went on like this for an hour or so. Then they ran out of cloths with which to mop their wet cheeks.

Dry your eyes, girls, said the wife: what good does it do to blub? We must make a plan.

They sat with no words for a while. All they could think of was to be as brave as they could, as brave as their dad Bee, and to go to the dark place whence the beasts had come, see if they could find Bee there.

Each one knew she was pale with fear at the thought of such a trip in to the wild. They stood up, took their shields, spears, swords, harps and mead cups, plus a bag each of bread and fruit and nuts and one spare pair each of clean knicks.

Right, they said, though their knees shook a bit: let us be off. Let us go and find Dad.

Out from the hall they went. They made their way, step by step, day by day, to the far off wild, as dark as hell. No roads and no paths. Just the bleak moor. Now they were lost. No maps to help. They came to a cold place, where black trees bent by a lake of ice. The home of Ms Dell.

She rose up, the great beast, through the ice. She broke through it. She was ice cold, and huge, a shape to blot out the sky. Such a size. Such a weight. If you spoke back, she would fall on you with rage, crush you, and you would be dead. Such a mouth and such teeth! Slime on her jaws. Flames shot from her mouth. Ha! she cried in beast talk: you want my boy, do you? Tough luck. He is mine. I love him much too much to let him go out with girls like you. Then she gave a snap of her jaws. Girl flesh! Nice! A lunch fit for a beast! She ate up the wife of Bee, crunch, and girl one, crunch, and girl two, crunch.

Girl three ran off as fast as she could. She sat in the dark wood. Cold round her like a coat, and fear for a scarf. Tears fell down her face; drops of ice. What shall I do? What shall I do?

A bird on a branch near to her sang a small cold song. Girl three gave a sigh. She took her flask of mead out of her bag and took a sip. Then she had a bite of bread and fruit. Come on, girl, she said: you need to go on. That is what Dad would say. And first, to drive the fear from me, to get my heart up, I need to sing a lay. And so she took her harp out of her bag and made up a song: the lay of Bee, of her lost dad. Now her heart grew much more warm. Just get on with it, she sang. As her mum would have sung had she still been live.

Right. Come on now. Try to be brave.

She stood up. Put all her stuff back in to her bag. Set off on her quest. Where to? She did not have a clue. The point was to set off. No road. No track. No map. Here is the dark wood. In you go.

THE DEAD MOTHERS' CLUB

Death, that magician, plays mysterious conjuring tricks. One moment Louise's mother is there and the next she's not. A version of Hitchcock's film *The Lady Vanishes.* In this case, from her bed. A swish and rattle of curtains. A stripped mattress. Into her box she goes.

Louise can't understand it. How can so much life, such a force of presence, simply disappear? Louise's tears fill up the gap. They spring out unexpectedly, like showers in March. One moment she's buying onions in the greengrocer's, and the next she's remembering how her mother always sautéd calf's liver with a purée of onions and a splash of cognac, and then she's sobbing into her armful of vegetables, spotting the brown paper bags with wet. Pain works at her like a saw, cutting her in two. This trick of death's not done by mirrors; it's real. Death breaks Louise apart; dismembers her. She can't mend herself.

Her mother's death tips the world askew. Off balance. Once, her mother was the whole world. Louise grew up shaped by her, in relation to her, a force to be fought, adored, resisted, longed for. Now the sky cracks apart and the space pressing against Louise's back and shoulders feels empty and cold. She stumbles, as though she's lost the heel off one shoe. Coming home from the shops she trips over bits of broken pavement.

Clumsy as a five-year-old on her first day at primary school trying to negotiate a path across the busy playground, she lurches along streets. The world seizes her and shoves her about, the city crowds rearranged into new patterns of swirling movement that toss her in their currents. The world knocks her over, and then the world catches her again. She bumps into a man unloading pallets from a white van. Mind yer backs! he sings out: oopsadaisy! The newsagent calls to her as she goes past: where've you been all this time, darling? A young woman bank clerk says to her: have you been crying? The skin under your eyes looks all shiny and odd.

Her dear friends ring up, write cards and emails, come to visit. They pat her, hug her, counsel her: take care, go gently, look after yourself. Dutifully Louise eats her vegetables and fruit, goes for brisk walks, gets early nights. In public she wears the mask of good behaviour. In private she feels possessed by a voracious howling child. She drinks too much wine, to quiet that child. She snacks on pork pies late in the evening, biting the crisp pastry as though it's an enemy. She has weird dreams of dismemberment, flaying, can't bear getting up in the morning. She sleepwalks through her days at work in the bookshop, spending as much time in the stockroom as she dares, pretending to check invoices. She feels as though she's jumped off the cliff; hovering in mid-air; about to crash.

Stabbing at the phone with her forefinger, Louise rehearses what she needs to say. Oh hello, my mother's one of your tenants, I mean she was, only she's died, I've been clearing out her house, I know you'll need it back, and now I'm ringing to organise how to get the keys to you.

Click. She stops. Realises she's speaking to a robot. The computerised voice, nasal female, sounds like one credit card tapping another. Press one. If you would like to speak to one of our advisers. Press two. Please hold. Muzak. Please hold. Bleep. At last, a human voice, muffled and faint. A sibyl down a cave. A grumpy sibyl, holding out little hope for the human race. Please speak up, cries Louise.

Friday at the latest, says the housing association sibyl: we'll expect the keys back before the office closes at five.

Sorry, Louise says: can't do that. I'll be at work. I'll come on Sunday to do my final clean-up and then I'll leave the keys with the neighbour.

She puts on her cleaning outfit: tracksuit bottoms, an old sweatshirt, trainers. These clothes make her feel dowdy and depressed so she takes them off and dons her new apple-green skirt, knee-length and full, and a skinny cardigan striped pink, red, pale green, pale blue. Hannah's kitchen is stuffed with aprons. She'll wear one of those over the top.

She takes the tube to the far end of the Metropolitan Line. Halt. A brick wall, hung with baskets of plastic petunias, rears up smash in front; just like death. Hannah believed you dissolved and passed through it, to the heavenly terminus on the other side. Jesus works the points and keeps you on track and then God the station-master welcomes you with open arms. No waiting room in purgatory for her. I've done all my suffering on earth, she tells Louise: I don't need any more punishment.

The little council estate hides behind the wooden fence on the far side of the local park. Louise dawdles, putting off the moment when she must enter her mother's house for the last time.

The suburb recaptures her in the net of family. Memory springs alive, devours her, turns her back into the child who wanted to be invisible, not to speak. Melting into the drowsy warmth of an August afternoon. Time hovers, ceases, the walk home stretches out, her feet drag over hot, glittering paving slabs. The smell of soft tarmac, its black glisten. An occasional car squelches past. The invisible ice-cream van tinkles its chimes about the avenues lined with ornamental cherry trees. Plump lawns with green stripes. Aeroplanes purr high overhead.

She wanders down the oak-lined avenue bisecting the

park. On one side of the wide path families sprawl on the rough long grass under the oak trees, watching a cricket match, the women in bright saris and the men in long white shirts, and around the edges of the park meadow the brick walls sheltering the backs of half-timbered mansionettes stand deep in hollyhocks and delphiniums that have escaped from the gardens and scrambled into wilderness. Toc-toc-toc of racket and ball on the nearby tennis courts.

On summer Sundays in childhood, after church and after lunch, when the outside world sulks beyond their dark creosoted fence, her parents rest on the chintz-covered cushions of the swing-seat set on the square of crazy-paving behind their kitchen, and drink tea. Post-war paradise: their own semi-detached two-bedroomed council house. A village-style estate: 1920s cottages arranged around a green, wedge-shaped gardens behind. Louise's father plants up the raw earth plot: Solomon's Seal and lilies of the valley in the front, a pear tree and gooseberry bushes at the back. He mulches and composts. He weeds. He clips, prunes, trims.

Hannah in widowhood lets the garden sprawl, relax. During her last year of life she doesn't bother with it at all. Louise keeps things in check for her, for a few months, then lets them slide. Hannah says: oh don't bother with the gardening, come back inside, come and talk to me.

Louise, arriving in front of her mother's little house, feels impressed at her own wilful neglect. How has she managed to uphold the rights to thrive of dandelions and plantain and nettles? How has she not succumbed to tidying things up? The front strip, more of a bed than a garden, a jostle of self-seeded sycamores, wild tussocks of grass, new growth of brambles sprouting bright green, ground elder, swarms against the pebble-dashed front wall. Overgrown shrubs almost hide the shabby window frames' peeling paint. Louise relishes the untidiness; so different from the front gardens on either side set with bedding plants in rainbow stripes lined up like obedient children. Hannah's house nurtures rebels, good robust weeds claiming space and sunshine. Hannah, lifelong devotee of neatness, in her last year liked the wildness. Nobody could see into the house. She sat behind a green veil of creepers, in green dimness.

How strange to step inside the tiny hall and embrace not Hannah but nothingness. Louise hovers. Not quite nothingness; not yet. A haziness in the air, a palpable coolness, like a damp cobweb laid on her neck. The little house smells cold and dusty. Emptiness forms a presence, hovering, wanting to scold. What d'you think you're doing, barging in like this? Louise braces herself to get on with this last bit of clearing up. It feels disrespectful, somehow, disturbing the atmosphere, tidying Hannah away. She delays, making herself a cup of milkless tea and standing with it in the middle of the postage-stamp sitting-room, staring at the patch on the faded orange wall where her mother's poster of Chartres Cathedral used to hang. Hannah gave it to the parish priest before she died. It leaves behind a square of brightness.

When your mother dies, you dispose of her bit by bit. You don't want to get rid of her but you do. It happens in stages. At each stage, inside yourself, you shout no no no I don't want to let go. Louise strokes Hannah's waxy yellow cheek. Hannah-not-Hannah. She pats her mother's white wicker coffin just before it slides behind the crematorium curtain while the organ attempts *Für Elise.* She pokes around her little house: Mum, where are you? Come out! She's a pirate, clambering aboard her mother's ship, ransacking her treasure chests. Finding a cargo of old cheque-book stubs, pension book, post-office savings book, bills, bank statements. Tatty old corn-dollies, withered bouquets of dried honesty and statice, half-used boxes of tissues, empty margarine tubs, scraps of soap, broken necklaces, single clip-on earrings, old theatre programmes, laddered tights, leaflets advertising special offers, church magazines, worn toothbrushes.

She packs clothes, costume jewellery, ornaments and books into boxes for the local charity shop, and then pots and pans and furniture, everything still in reasonable shape, into the dealer's van. They jam in together like refugees.

Some of the pieces are classics, in their way. A 1950s tallboy. A wardrobe from the 1920s: a poor person's version of Arts and Crafts. Easy chairs from the 1960s. Louise runs her hand over the front of the tallboy. Pale walnut veneer. Two drawers above panelled doors concealing paper-lined shelves. Ridged horizontal handles in the same wood. That tallboy held her childhood. She kept her clothes in it for eighteen years.

She doesn't want to let all Hannah's things go. If ever she could afford to move somewhere a bit bigger than her little flat, she'd like to hang onto some of Hannah's stuff. She'd like to sit tête à tête with a friend in those two armchairs, stack sheets and tea-towels in that tallboy, hang her clothes in that odd little wardrobe, whip egg whites with that wheel-driven whisk, make purée with that potato masher. When she and Hannah found it hard to love one another they exchanged words hard-edged as metal tools, clanging blade on blade; weapons that hurt. Two toddlers banging each other's boiled eggs with fierce spoons. Each other's skulls. Perhaps women learn how to fight in kitchens, using kitchen tools. Kitchen warriors trying to slaughter each other with ice-cream scoops and saucepan lids. Louise wants that worn-down wooden spoon, that enamel ladle, that double-handled half-moon cutter. She puts them into her bag. She adds the lidded porcelain sweet-pot that always stood on the table by Hannah's chair.

The dealer deliberates. He gets out his chequebook from the pocket of his leather jacket. I'll give you a hundred pounds for the lot. Louise says: done! Together they finish loading the van. The dealer leaves, shouting cheerio.

The house still seems full. Louise keeps opening built-in cupboards, hidden in eaves, she's forgotten to check on her previous visits, and discovering more stuff. The debris of Hannah's life surrounds her. As though Hannah were the house, and death has knocked it down, scattered Hannah in bits.

Today Louise must get on with her final task; collect up the leftover bits and pieces, regard them, name them, attach meaning to them, decide whether to throw them away or give them away. She must discriminate between rubbish and possible souvenirs but she doesn't know how to do it. The biscuit tin decorated with a worn stencil of the Coronation, in which Hannah stored bags of low-fat potato crisps. The tapestry picture of a bouquet of flowers, intended as a cushion-cover perhaps, which Hannah left half-finished. Her bottles of pills. Her blue and orange crocheted bedspread. Her chipped yellow teapot and knitted brown tea-cosy. Her piles of neatly ironed face flannels. Louise feels like an archaeologist, digging and brushing and dusting fragments of Hannah's life, sorting and combing, labelling and packing. She'll bear them away into the museum of her memory and make sense of them later on.

She opens the kitchen drawer and selects her favourite of Hannah's hand-made aprons. Tiny dark blue checks, pockets and bib edged with dark blue braid, gathered into a waistband, long blue ties. Wearing this apron she feels like a housewife in a 1950s magazine. Or in a modern ad: retro-chic. Now she's ready to collect up the very last of the clutter and junk, thrust it into black bin bags. The Christmas decorations: paper chains and pleated tissue-paper bells and ropes of tinsel. Old icing-bags and sheets of greaseproof paper, the plastic spatula melted at one corner, the scratched non-stick frying pan, handle gold with ancient burnt-on grease, the dried cakes of shoe polish, wreaths of rubber bands, rolls of vouchers and coupons for special offers, all out of date. Louise packs them into the big plastic sacks.

What a pile of tack, eh? Hannah jokes.

Louise jumps and drops the pile of old vests she's been holding. Oh Mum, she says: you know I don't think you're rubbish, you know I hate throwing your stuff away.

She wants to discover loving letters addressed to herself, tie up bulky bundles of caresses and conversations, cram Hannah into a suitcase and take her home, she wants Hannah not to be dead. Fat tears rush out of her eyes and roll down her face. She puts aside a few more mementoes: Hannah's cookery book; her best lace-edged handkerchief; her three best tea-towels, blue-striped cream linen, smoothed and worn by use, loops at the corners, cotton labels bearing Hannah's initials in curly red lettering. Louise shakes out then re-folds the tea-towels. All her life Hannah used them solely for drying-up glasses. Cotton tea-towels of the second rank, printed with faded rustic scenes, souvenirs from visits to stately homes, wiped plates and saucepans. Louise screws these into balls, uses them as dusters.

Cloths stand for sensuality. Soft as a mother's skin. Cloths stand in for your mother's hands stroking you. You can stroke them even when your mother's vanished; you can dry-up with them as carefully as she did. No shattered glasses. No splinters. Louise likes inheriting these treasures. She's already got Hannah's pale blue leather handbag stowed away at home. Now, cleaning her mother's house, the wallpaper of the empty rooms swagged with spiders' webs, she kneels to brush the edges of the carpet close to the walls, the way Hannah always did. As Louise coaxes tufts of grey fluff into her dustpan Hannah remarks: well, you never were much good at housework, I'm surprised you're managing this at all. Louise says: oh Mum, you underestimate me, I can do housework when I want to. She moves through the bare space with vacuum and sponge and bucket of hot soapy water. Hannah gives instructions: don't forget to clean behind the cooker. Don't forget to polish the taps. OK, Mum! says Louise.

She stacks the black bin bags, mop and brooms, and box of cleaning things outside the front door, bangs the door shut behind her. Let anyone who wants come and scavenge for this peerless upright Hoover with bandaged flex and grey imitation-tweed bag, this classic 1950s speckled grey enamel dustpan and matching brush. She pushes the keys through the neighbour's letter-box, as previously arranged, then hurries off down the road.

Louise puts off her next task. She has vanquished heaps of dust, spiders' webs and fluff but still she has one last clearing-up job left. She waits another week. Saturday passes. Sunday approaches. She decides. Today she'll do it. Accordingly she puts the lidded porcelain sweet-pot back into her bag and sets forth.

Where to go, exactly? Almost anywhere will do. Green enough, secluded enough. Not crowded. Might as well just stick a pin in a map. She alights from the tube at Euston. The carriage doors bump shut behind her. Groups of tourists clog the platform, the exits. She edges patiently forwards. How about the raffish, scruffy district just north of here? Wastelands and scrap yards, sheds and small businesses under railway arches, bridges and gasworks. A surprising oasis of roughness in the smoothed-out city centre. Earmarked for development, which means it will all get torn down. Another bit of urban history destroyed.

She hesitates. Shrugs. Come on. Just get out of the station building and walk, find an abandoned corner, overgrown with wild buddleia and rose bay willow herb. That will do the trick. Just the ticket, as Hannah used to say.

Hey, says Hannah: why have you got off here? Hey, says Louise: I didn't know you were still talking to me.

Louise darts up the escalator, silver step to silver step, emerges into the light. Mum, you stay underground. That's where you belong, in the underworld.

On the Euston Road she hovers at the kerb. Blue sky curves above like a tent in a fairground. She feels loose: an untethered balloon. Some sort of umbilical cord's been cut. London opens up: she could go anywhere, be anything. She could just fly off and never come back. No one to hold her string; she's a divorcée kite, a motherless kite, a childless kite, whirled up on gusts of wind.

She starts to wander, loop about. She avoids the main road's traffic fumes, noise, pollution haze. She plays a game of letting herself get lost. No map and no *A to Z*. She dives down backstreets she doesn't know, chooses to turn aside at whim, to follow her nose, to let herself be diverted. She's a vagrant, zigzagging, open to adventure.

She dips down into the district just south of Kings Cross, into streets lined with shabby small hotels. Men loaf outside, smoking. A girl erupts from the doorway of one unmarked house, pelts full-tilt down the stone steps, onto the pavement. She almost barges into Louise, who swerves, jerks aside to protect her bag. Hey! A fury of feet, clenched fists, swirl of yellow ra-ra skirt. Very thin. Tight pale face. Firing herself out into the day like a rocket. She charges off along the street, turns the corner, disappears. Eddies of fear in her wake. Does that girl need rescuing? She's gone. Vanished.

Louise makes her feet change track. She meanders eastwards, through northern Clerkenwell and Finsbury. Something tugs her along: the right place to pause hides just ahead. Her route twists and turns and doubles back.

On Clerkenwell Road she slows down, to scan the windows of the old-fashioned Italian delis, the sign advertising the Italian driving-school. She stops outside a wide church façade, nineteenth-century and ornate, wedged in between two buildings. High railings, padlocked, defend the steps up to the big doors. St Peter's Church. The Italian church in Clerkenwell.

Her mother brought her here once, in childhood, to show her where she'd attended Mass as a girl, where she'd got married. Glittering baroque interior, ice-blue walls, aisles studded with carved stands supporting brightly-coloured statues of saints; the choking smell of incense. Two ladies in flowered overalls swirl mops across opposite ends of the pink marble sanctuary floor, shout cheerfully to one another as they work through lakes of soapsuds. They treat the sacred men-only space as just another kitchen.

Hannah calls hello. The cleaning ladies look up and cry out in surprise. They dart across the wet, shining slabs, push through the low gate set in the sanctuary railings. They kiss Hannah, exclaim volubly over Louise in hoarse voices. She stares at her toecaps.

The ladies abandon their buckets, lead the visitors into the taboo space. A curtain draws aside; a little back door, previously hidden, opens in the curved wall behind the high golden altar. Louise enters a secret place. Like another room inside your flat that you find in a dream, a room that you didn't know existed. Down a dark narrow corridor they file, into the priest's house. Old and high-ceilinged, smelling of incense and snuffed candles, as though the church is trying to creep in. The panelled dining-room holds wooden armchairs set around a big table covered with a white lace-edged cloth. The ladies run to fetch glasses and plates, pour brown liquid, serve hard almond biscuits, tongue-shaped, that you dip into the sweet wine. *Vin santo*, the priest says. His scanty grey hair reveals his scalp. His amused mouth curves upwards. Brown eyes round as raisins. A long black dress. He chats to Hannah, then makes the sign of the cross over Louise. Dunking his biscuit he seems human, not like a priest at all, seems to like being surrounded by women all talking at once. He lets them out of his front door, down steps into a side street round the corner from the church, and waves goodbye.

At the bus-stop, Hannah clicks her tongue. Not a dining-room, silly: that was the sacristy. All those cupboards are full of vestments.

Louise knows: green for ordinary Sundays, purple for Lent and Advent, white for joy. Brocade copes embroidered with costly gold thread. The priest dresses up for his parishioners; their Sunday doll. All through the week he just wears black. Then on Sundays he throws off his disguise and bursts out into colour: a magical totem suddenly displaying his true costume. On his reverent back he bears clothes that talk, that say rejoice, that say now mourn, now feel forgiven, now sing. So much more articulate than her father's clothes, his dark weekday suit, his weekend cardigans, beige cable-knit with wooden buttons.

Is that why Louise has put on her green skirt again today? No black and no purple; time to recover and be ordinary, going about the world, going about her business through the hurrying crowds. The crowds close around that desperate running girl. She vanishes. Becomes lost in the mass. Yet every single person is distinct. Together they make up vast migrating crowds of animals fleeing across dusty plains, galloping along all together, exquisitely adjusted to each other, not bumping into each other, flowing along, knowing they've got to move, to change. The one and the many, the one in the many. You're merged in the city crowd and yet you're still yourself. The herd is one sleek animal and Louise is part of the herd and she is one small animal like all the other animals just going along doing what has to be done and so is that girl.

She turns off Clerkenwell Road, wide, too busy with traffic. She strolls through alleys, narrow streets, tiny squares linked by flights of stone steps. The city reveals itself to her like a dreamscape; she's lived in it all her life but today she's finding out its secrets afresh. The city expands as she goes deeper into it. The city opens up inside her mind. The cold breeze and the hot sun polish her face.

Lovely day for an outing, says her mother: oh I do like

getting out for a breath of fresh air. Louise says: I thought I'd shaken you off. You were supposed to stay behind down on the tube.

Louise hurries around a corner. She catches a waft of bittersweet perfume: sun-heated leaves of box and bay. She walks through a narrow passage between high stone walls, emerges into a pocket of green surrounded by railings, terraced houses. A black and white sign at the iron gate set in the railings names it All Saints' Place. The little notice board alongside bears an explanatory poster: the former parish church of All Saints' having been demolished, the church's graveyard became this public park.

The foursquare street frames a little garden: flowerbeds planted with domed clumps of white and purple lace-cap hydrangeas, myrtle. From her plinth a battered stucco nymph, stooping over the pleated stone stole she draws around her thighs, her shoulders dark with green lichen, supervises a small wooden bench. Surrounding the garden, enclosing it, late eighteenth-century houses pack in tight together. On one side the terrace runs along a raised pavement, a steep little flight of steps, railed-in, reaching up to it at either end.

Nice, says her mother: very nice. Let's stop here for a bit, shall we? Have a rest. I'm worn out with all this careering about.

Outside one house, in the middle of the raised terrace, rears a red For Sale sign. Blue front door, the paint faded and blistered. Blue window-box sprouts dry stalks. A neat little Georgian dolls-house. Louise gazes, daydreams. Kitchen, sitting-room, bedroom, piled one on top of each other like children's bricks; all for me. No, don't be daft, I'd never be able to afford it. Envy slashes her insides to red ribbons.

Time for a sit-down, says her mother: let's find a café, shall we? I'm dying for a nice cup of tea.

The low wrought-iron gate, standing half open, gives access to the square garden. In goes Louise. Tall trees at one side shade a line of ancient tombstones, collected up and set in a row, half-toppled in long grass. They seem to be growing there like strange ivory-coloured plants, rounded and stubby, as alive as teeth in a baby's gums. The mouth of the garden talks to her; tombstone teeth are alive and chew on the living. Oh yes, Mum, mutters Louise: I've always known that.

She treads across the green turf to examine the tombstones. She crouches in front of them, peering at their mossy inscriptions. They seem like tall books. Decorated letters and cards from long ago; the dead wanting to speak to her, pushing up their pale stone thumbs: hey you! Her eye strokes their scrolled tops, their carved ornamental reliefs of solemn cherubs and skulls-and-bones, their cut lettering.

The church is long gone. Louise is gone too; fallen; sunk down beneath London houses, London pavements, London streets. A fine little neo-classical church,

All Saints' must once have been, with plain glass windows and oak pews; a holy submarine cruising the sewers and the underground tunnels of the city. The parson in his black coat and white bands clutches the edge of his pulpit, his ship's wheel, steers his church-boat, his stone ark, down through the dark layers of history, down to a mulch of broken Saxon pots, fragments of wicker coffins, drifts of human ashes, shards of animal bones, down to that place where everybody becomes part of everybody else; part of mud, part of coal. The dead don't know they're coal and they don't care.

But I'm not dead yet. She blinks, comes back up to ground level. She opens her shoulder-bag and extracts the cardigan wrapping the porcelain sweet-pot. She peels off the sellotape fastening the lid in place, lifts off the lid. Grey feathers of ash her fingers brush into a heap. She licks her forefinger, dips it in. Tastes. Gritty nothingness. Holy communion mum. A choir of cleaning-ladies with mops will sing you into sanctuary. She pours the ashes out among the tombstones. Goodbye, Mum.

The air takes the grains of dust, shifts them about. A ruffle of cloud. Some sticks on her face and she wipes it off with the back of her hand, tears and ashes and snot all mixed up. She puts the pot back in her bag.

Where are you where are you? Hannah's voice fades, as though she's crying out from a long way off. Deep mud bed. She has sunk down with the other dead people.

Louise has buried her, forced her under the earth, tucked the graveyard around her like a blanket, held her down while she struggles. Sssh, be quiet.

Hannah calls: Louise, don't leave me here, I don't like it. She wails like a child. Louise wants to pick her mother up, rock her, soothe her. No, no, of course you're not going to die. No, the cancer's operable. No, I won't abandon you, I'll take care of you, I'll stay with you. She touches a tombstone, passing her hand over its rough lichened top, yellowy-green. Oh Mum, please try to understand, you belong down there now, that's all. Down with all the other dead mothers. In the dead mothers' club.

She walks back onto the path, approaches the centre of the garden. Next to the stone nymph stands an urn planted with trailing clematis; dark blue flowers flaring open like gargoyle faces. They roar at her: death will come soon enough for you too. Nearby, unpruned lilac trees show brown flowers, withered cones ending in sharp points.

Louise sits down on the bench. No hurry. She can exist in this moment, the heat of the sun pressing on her face and under the heat the coolness of a breeze starting up, the two layers together first enfolding her and then pushing her out of her skin, making her dissolve into the daylight, the golden air sweet and tart as Seville oranges. She never could make marmalade as good as her mother's. She curls her fingers round the edge of the bench. She feels like a child who's been set some difficult homework. No mother she can ask for help. That's the whole point. She grapples with a knowledge which keeps sliding away.

The body which once sheltered her has gone. A skin stripped off. A sheltering cover pulled back, the sky peeled to rags. The world feels raw. Geography's changed. Time's changed. All her life she's lived inside her mother, somehow, and now she's been born a second time but she can't yet sit up, she can't walk. She can't talk properly. Just blurted, disconnected words. Stabbed stomach, hot eyes spurting tears, a need to bend forwards hands clasped around herself and howl.

Death. Hide-and-seek mother. Now you see her now you don't. Her silkworm mother weaves a case of silk. Her mother's self falls away from her like a carapace, a chrysalis. Louise crawls out with wet wings. Her mother is the wetness on her wings. Her mother is the wetness on her face. Tears pour down her cheeks. She lets them. On your own in a park, you can cry freely; you don't need to worry about upsetting other people. You don't have to stop crying in order to console them for your upset. The tears acknowledge the simple truth: Hannah's dead.

Louise yawns. She fishes for her handkerchief and mops her eyes, blows her nose. She leaves the square and walks south. She carries her mother, light as a communion wafer, inside her, the ghost of an ancestor.

On the Beach at Trouville

Abstract

White shapes. Splashes of white in the foreground, thick wide brushstrokes of white oil paint. A shape of white put into the world, a shape that wasn't there before. Babies' souls are white except for the dark stain of original sin; the human fingerprint. But this white paint is all material. Paintflesh. Voluptuous. It draws Thérèse closer.

The picture's not whole, doesn't offer a coherent story. It keeps breaking up into bits. A blue shape, geometrical, which refers to something called a parasol. A blue star? It exists in two dimensions and in three. On the right, an odd black hexagram, chopped off. Thérèse asks: what's that? The painter shrugs: don't know yet. Wait and see.

In between these forms: a curving shape of whiteness,

greyness, creaminess, that Thérèse can call the sky, the beach; its base finishing in that white blaze. A ruffle on the cuff of a dress: just an excuse for one thick stroke of pale blue-white paint.

A curling run of white denotes a frill.

A line of white also means light falling onto the top and back of a chair. Two white triangles suggest turned-down collar tips. White smudges can denote a glove, a book – if the painter wants them to.

Thérèse backs away, one hand curling to a fist and the other gripping the handle of her parasol: the picture makes her feel smashed up inside. The man painting, the woman seated opposite his easel, nod at her. Don't run away. Do sit down. The man's slippery glance travels along Thérèse's bare arm while his fingers wipe a brush on a rag, smoothe oil onto cloth. Wind hurls itself inland, scoops up sand, blows it into her face, stinging. Wet grit sticks to her eyelids, her mouth. Therese stabs the tip of her parasol into the sand. She turns, gropes her way back up the beach to the family group waiting for her on the promenade. Her aunt's skirts balloon out and she holds them down, laughing. Her uncle tucks Thérèse's arm into his: we don't want you getting blown away!

Autobiography

Thérèse fingers the notebook and pencil in her pocket. She wants to shape her life into the story of her search for

God. She'll delay writing her autobiography as long as possible, while she perfects herself. Then she'll be able to perfect the writing, carve chapters sparkling as sugar. How will she write from the perspective of the convent? Climbing onto a wooden stool, pulling apart the shutters, she'll peer down from the high little window of her cell at the tops of the brick arches of the cloister; angles rather than curves. If she leans right out, she'll be able to see a few leafless rose bushes, the stone cross at the intersection of the gravel paths bisecting the cloister garth. A space of emptiness the nuns fill with God. A wall separates the convent from the streets of Lisieux, thick with shops selling velour hats adorned with bunches of wax grapes, fur stoles, velvet boots, be-ribboned boxes of chocolates, corsets stiffened with whalebone, gold-frogged coats, tasselled cushions, embroidered antimacassars, flounced curtains. The nuns wear sandals and no stockings. Each unheated cell contains a bed, a stool, a lamp, a jug. Into the convent though, Thérèse will bring her memories. Vowing herself to poverty, she won't be able to strip away her past. Begin with childhood, then.

Summer holidays stretch out like the beach. Motherless time never ends. Mothers slip like sand through Thérèse's fingers: birth mothers, foster mothers, godmothers. At her fingertip touch the hourglass tilts; sand runs through; repeatedly. Mothers like grains of sand vanish: into death; back onto the farm; into the convent. Cliffs tumble, grind each other to rock, pebbles, sand.

Thérèse's older sister, the nun, whom Thérèse visits on Sundays, explains: each soul is one grain of sand and God loves each of us individually, particularly.

The sea drags shingle and sand from the beach and takes them away. Drowns them. Tides of loss that repeat, repeat. Water lashes Thérèse's eyes and her family reproach her for crying so often: such weakness, such self-indulgence. Where's your faith? Your mother's in heaven.

Life on earth means loneliness for ever. Bleakness that will never change. She'll teeter on the edge of the wind-scoured cliff and nobody will care that she tilts forward like the hourglass, spins in mid-air, smashes onto the rocks, loses her insides. Just part of the sand on the beach nameless and faceless. No more suffering. An end to it. Earthly time drums on, her heartbeat pounding, the blood beating in her ears. She wants to kill time, eat it up, bite the hourglass. Her mouth will fill with shards, streams of blood.

Thérèse concentrates, focuses her will, rises above worldly time, out of the time of clocks and seasons, launches herself towards no-time, towards eternity. She will inhabit heaven, play in God's walled garden, be sheltered in God's house. God will never leave her. He's gentle and white-bearded, like her papa. He chooses her to be his little queen. Seated on God's lap, cuddling him, she commands the universe. Look, it's starting to rain, because I'm sad.

Her aunt and uncle declare: you need a summer holiday. Fourteen-year-old girls shouldn't be moping about at home. They hurry her off with them and their children to Trouville. The beach offers liberty to the troop of cousins: out here, watched by her indulgent relatives, Therese, if she chooses, can run, yell, dive in and out of the waves, invent new games in the water, explore caves, pick her way over the flat expanse of rocks at low tide, lie on the beach in the sun. The beach offers the tang of the salt wind, the smell of salt water, the taste of salt on her lips. A spread rug delineates home. For their picnic tea her aunt produces chunks of crusty baguette with sticks of dark chocolate rammed down inside them, and gritty lemonade out of a tin flask. Then the children race away again. Thérèse's aunt repacks the basket. Her uncle collapses into a doze.

Thérèse takes off her boots, rolls her stockings down. She walks barefoot over the flat expanse of sand towards the distant, shining line of the sea. She allows herself to paddle at the water's edge. A shock of cold water: strokes of hot sun. She discards her tight little black jacket, rolls up the black sleeves of her blouse. The air caresses her bare arms. Her aunt does not come paddling but remains sitting on the beach, fully dressed; sewing. There are times when women don't swim. Thérèse connects those times to the fluttering flag whose colour denotes the state of the water, the waves. Green means safe to swim, yellow means be careful. Red signals danger. Red rags mean the loss of liberty, the loss of the sea's freedom. Thérèse's aunt wears a grey dress flecked with mauve and lilac. Half-mourning, to commemorate her sister's birthday. Women who wear black are widows. On Sundays back in Lisieux the church fills with their tides of black crepe frocks and black crepe veils. Washing in along the pews. Thérèse's mother wore a white frock with blue polka dots. She was invincible; for a time. She was the queen; for a time. Until cancer got her and she died.

Annunciation

Going to church, learning to be a Catholic, means learning about time; the past tense; the story of how everything began and then went wrong. Human beings get a second chance when God tips the hourglass so that time will begin again. A new story. The birth of a baby. God sends his angel to announce to Mary he's chosen her to become the baby's mother. Sometimes in paintings the angel arrives as a ribbon of words, a waving banner. Sometimes as a whisper brushing Mary's ear. Sometimes as a beam of light. God's decision falls into his chosen one's lap in a blaze of radiance. Camille on honeymoon walks out onto the bright beach, seats herself on a canvas chair. The light pools in her lap. The light laps her. The light lies in her lap like a lover. Her husband buries his face in her lap. He paints the light worshipping her knees. He's the light caressing her layers of muslin, he's the wind ruffling up her creamy petticoats. Camille, the young bride, wears her new hat, adorned with red, blue, purple anemones, bought for the honeymoon. In the painting in church the Virgin Mary wears a crown of bright flowers. Dressed only in garlands of golden leaves she lopes into Camille's dreams, tangles herself into Camille's mind. Camille sits and remembers her dream of the night before, imagines the night to come. Smiling, she'll grasp his arms, she'll say slow down what's the hurry? She hovers in the light and the brightness between two nights, two shapes of darkness. She holds her desire inside herself; pulsing between her legs. When she's ready she'll get up, shake sand from her skirts, turn to her husband, suggest it's time for lunch. She'll order moules à la marinière. While other diners use knife and fork she'll tear open the gleaming blue and black shells with her fingers and toss back cold Muscadet and call for more bread to mop up the juices. Between her lips, onto her tongue, between her teeth: plump yellow mussels scented with wine, garlic, parsley and seawater. Then up the narrow curving stairs of the boarding house she'll scamper with her husband, tugging him into their shuttered room, a dazzle of white sheets, and they'll unpeel each other's layers of clothes and she'll lay him out flat and kiss him all over and then turn head to tail so they can suck each other while the salt wind blows in from the sea, billowing out the long white lace curtains.

Cool air caresses their hot skin. Gulls scream, tumble past the window, their wings white as Camille's rounded stomach.

At midday, against the scorch of the sun she lifts her parasol. She gazes wordlessly from under its blue shade. A blue star shines in daylight. She shelters under a blue roof, inside soft walls of blue light. Soft blue veils drop down around her.

Monet gazes at Camille. This calm, majestic woman, his wife, part of the pale, light-bleached landscape, reminds him of Piero della Francesca's image of the pregnant Madonna pointing at the slit in her gown, the swell of the baby dancing inside. Two angels, one on each side, hold aside the flaps of the tent, the flaps of the Madonna's cloak. She draws down her blue blinds, closes her blue doors. Camille closes her eyes. Monet picks up a slender brush, taps Camille's nose with it: hey, daydreamer, sit up straight, will you?

Blue

The painting's a monochrome study; a monochrome in blue. The blue of the sea collects under Camille's parasol. She's cut the blue from the sky, leaving just a shred in the upper left hand corner, and stitched and stretched it to give herself blue shade.

In Normandy it rains a lot in summer. Grey sky, white clouds, patches of blue. Therese watches the sky from her bedroom window. The servant-girl crossing the gravel below looks up, spots her and shouts: just enough blue to make a pair of sailor's trousers! Thérèse calls back: no, a cloak for the Virgin! She wants to don a pair of clogs like the servant girl's, go out into the blue-grey drizzle, rock through mud, feel wet on her face, spin round and dance and shriek. Instead, she sits back down at her desk and carries on painting the holy picture she began yesterday. A miniature in water-colour, depicting the Holy Child Jesus holding a ball. Plump, curly-haired and beaming, he's offering it to his pink-cheeked chum Thérèse: will you be my little ball, let me kick you toss you pierce you abandon you in a corner? Thérèse breathes: yes. She slides her hand into her apron pocket, touches the string of loose beads she keeps there. A discipline taught her by her older sister the nun. She slips one bead along the string, to mark her gesture of self-denial in not going out to play in the rain; knots the bead into place. Come Sunday, she'll count up her acts of sacrifice, record her week's tally in her little blue notebook. When she visits her sister in the convent parlour on Sunday afternoon to give her the picture she'll tell her these memory-beads and her sister will stretch her hand through the grille and pat her. Skin reddened and cracked from the laundry. Bitten fingernails. Her sister will say: even on holiday at Trouville you'll find occasions for self-discipline, just you wait and see. Thérèse stares at her sister's head bandaged in a white coif, a kind of bag enclosing her face, pulled well down over her forehead, cutting off her eyebrows; at the black veil clumsily pinned round it. She whispers: my aunt says I'm to have a new summer outfit. I'll be obedient and wear it. That's my mortification!

Her sister says: make sure it's black, though, *ma chérie*.

Clouds

On the beach the sky whips with white and grey clouds. Wind races off the sea, buffets Monet as he paints rapidly. The skirts of his jacket flap. Sand whirls around his easel. Its legs rock. He curses, puts out a hand. Stabs his brush into blue, dances it onto the canvas. Dabs darker blue on the parasol rim and ribs, Camille's cuffs, a couple of folds on her dress. A blue flower in her hat. Blue indicates the time for dreaming, imagining. Camille lives in blue time. *L'heure bleue*, when the sky changes day into evening. Radiant blue darkness.

Monet paints a second young woman, seated opposite Camille. Who is she, this girl in black? He doesn't care; sharp-edged, she suits his composition, and that's what matters. Her back to the sun, her parasol tipped against light and heat, her face stays in shadow. Downcast eyes, gloved hands holding a book. She reads intently. A novel? A railway timetable? She and Camille sit together as calmly as old friends. She rests in Camille's presence and Camille rests in hers; one of them dissolved in reading, the other dissolved in her own reverie. The white light connects them, splashing onto Camille's frock, sliding across the back of the chair, touching the edge of the page of Thérèse's book. The light knots them together in a white net of secret thoughts. Monet's sucked breath whistles through his teeth: nearly done.

Camille decides that she'll invite the girl to join Monet and herself for lunch. She wants a witness of her happiness. Once a painting's finished, packed up, sold, who cares about the model? She needs to be appreciated now, this moment. Camille needs Thérèse to raise her eyes and admire a blissful married couple. Monet will eat with an appetite to match hers, he'll crack jokes to make them laugh and speak with his mouth full and their words will flip-flop across the tabletop lively as silver-blue-black mackerel. Then she and Monet will bid Thérèse goodbye and go upstairs for their siesta, roll about under a billowy white quilt, pelt each other with fat white pillows until the linen cover splits and feathers fly out, float to the floor.

Darkness

A black cloud blots out the sun. The sudden chilliness makes Camille jump. Looking at the black-clad girl seated opposite her, she shivers. Thérèse whispers: no, I can't. Camille frowns: so rude. What's wrong with her? She glares at the gawky girl. Thérèse seems suddenly threatening; like a ghost come to warn of approaching death. She has materialised on the beach like a self Camille's forgotten, a child howling with nightmare, wetting the bed, sleepwalking downstairs to find someone to make everything all right. Thérèse is a black tide flooding in. She'll pour herself into Camille and make her cry. Camille begins to loosen, her edges start to flow out, she could be anyone, anything. Who am I? What's a self? She might get lost, never get back to herself. She wants Monet to paint neat black lines around her, holding her in; to paint a chair between herself and the girl in black; like bars. Keep off. Don't touch me. Yes of course she knows who she is. My name is Camille Monet. She knows what her life will be like. Happiness with her dear husband. A child. A house, a garden with fruit trees, kitchen shelves laden with copper pans and jars of apricot jam, a stove faced with blue and white patterned porcelain tiles. Blue as the paint on Monet's brush.

Dreams

Mid-morning. The family goes out for a stroll. Thérèse leaves her aunt and uncle on the promenade, descends the flight of wooden steps onto the beach, sits down on the grey-yellow sand. She tries to concentrate on reading the notes she has scribbled in her diary but the sun dazzles on the pages, makes her squint. Too much light. Too much beach, too much sea. Once she has entered the convent, where her black-swathed sister waits for her, she will swear never to leave, never to try and see the sea again. She'll be sand in God's mortar and he can grind her to dust. Aged sixteen, she will walk from the public section of the convent chapel into a dark, tiled vault, knock at the enclosure door, kneel, wait for permission to enter. She will explode with joy, shoot up to heaven like a firework, spin like a mad hourglass, like a Catherine wheel dropping gobbets of fire, shower her mother with gold and silver grains of stars.

She doesn't dare swim. The sea throws itself at her and she fears that it will suck her in, drown her. Salt tears. And yet she longs to jump in. God's there. Her mother's there. Fall off the cliff and let them catch you. Leap. Trust. Let go. Fall out of time. She hovers on the beach, tilting herself back and forth between the sea and the land.

Two more years of daylight. Aged fourteen, strolling the shoreline at Trouville, hatless, skirts tucked up, wearing a black muslin blouse open at the neck, sleeves rolled up to the shoulder, she catches the painter's eye. Wanders across. The painter and his wife invite her to sit down. Camille pats the empty canvas seat next to her own: do join us. I'm in need of company. Stay and talk to me while he finishes his painting. Thérèse says: what's it of? She peers at it. Oh.

The young woman in a bulk of white muslin and the

young woman in black, seated together on the beach; the glimmering expanse of wet sand stretching out behind them; the incoming tide. Separate ends of the monochromatic scale and in between them blue and blue-grey and dark blue and indigo.

PAPER HOUSES

Michèle Roberts

Michèle Roberts, one of Britain's most talented and highly acclaimed novelists, considers her own life, in this vibrant, powerful portrait of a time and place: alternative London of the 1970s and beyond. A fledgling writer taking a leap into radical politics, Roberts finds alternative homes, new families and lifelong friendships in the streets and houses of Holloway, Peckham, Regent's Park and Notting Hill Gate. From *Spare Rib* to publishing her first book, *Paper Houses* is Roberts' story of finding a space in which to live, love and write – and learning to share it.

'Beguiling, enthusiastic, charming and vivid, this is an autobiography to be savoured'
Amanda Craig, *Daily Telegraph*